"Give me the amulet!"

"The amulet!" he said, and his voice was the same voice that had come out of nowhere a moment earlier. "Give me the amulet!"

"No!" she screamed. "I can't!"

She tried to draw away from him, but his arms were tight about her, hot and scaly and smelling of death. She beat at his chest and her hands sank right into it.

They burned.

"The amulet," he said again. His eyes were pits of fire now, his nose an upturned horror with ragged nostrils in the middle of his scaly face. He opened his mouth and a forked tongue flickered between yellow fangs. "Give me the amulet!"

When she refused he lowered his head toward her neck. She could feel hot breath, and the drip of burning saliva . . .

Books by Bruce Coville

The A.I. Gang Trilogy

Operation Sherlock
Robot Trouble
Forever Begins Tomorrow

Bruce Coville's Alien Adventures

Aliens Ate My Homework
I Left My Sneakers in Dimension
The Search for Snout

Camp Haunted Hills

How I Survived My Summer Vacation
Some of My Best Friends Are Monsters
The Dinosaur That Followed Me Home

Magic Shop Books

Jennifer Murdley's Toad
Jeremy Thatcher, Dragon Hatcher
The Monster's Ring

My Teacher Books

My Teacher Is an Alien
My Teacher Fried My Brains
My Teacher Glows in the Dark
My Teacher Flunked the Planet

Space Brat Books

Space Brat
Space Brat 2: Blork's Evil Twin
Space Brat 3: The Wrath of Squat
Space Brat 4: Planet of the Dips

The Dragonslayers

Goblins in the Castle

Monster of the Year

Available from MINSTREL® Books

BRUCE COVILLE'S CHAMBER OF HORRORS

AMULET OF DOOM

AN ARCHWAY PAPERBACK
Published by POCKET BOOKS
New York London Toronto Sydney Tokyo Singapore

AN ARCHWAY PAPERBACK *Original*

An Archway Paperback published by
POCKET BOOKS, a division of Simon & Schuster Inc.
1230 Avenue of the Americas, New York, NY 10020

Copyright © 1985, 1996 by Bruce Coville

ISBN: 0-671-53637-0

First Archway Paperback printing February 1996

10 9 8 7 6 5 4 3 2 1

AN ARCHWAY PAPERBACK and colophon are
registered trademarks of Simon & Schuster Inc.

Front cover illustration by Ciruelo Cabral

Printed in the U.S.A.

IL 6+

For Diane and Paul

Introduction:
STEP INTO MY
CHAMBER

At the end of the street stands a strange old house. You check the address on the piece of yellowed paper you hold in your trembling hand. Yes, this is it. You've come to the right place. The chamber of horrors is straight ahead, waiting for you, waiting for you to enter.

You climb the rickety steps. The door creaks as you open it. A cobweb brushes your forehead, and from the corner of your eye you notice something with more legs than seems natural scuttle into the darkness.

In the shadows ahead lurks your host. He utters a low, mysterious, bone-chilling laugh.

And suddenly you wonder if this is really where you want to be.

You'd better turn back now, while you still can,

because your journey into the heart of fear is about to begin.

What's this? You're going to stay?

Well, then—welcome to my nightmares. I've been studying fear all my life. First my own fears, the creeping terrors that came at night and left me staring into the dark, wondering what lurked in the closet, under the bed, waiting to grab me, take me, carry me away. Then the fear I found in movies, and books, and (sometimes most delicious of all) around campfires. I experienced the thrill of the chill, and at the same time yearned to learn to do the same thing to others— to you, dear reader: to make your blood run cold with fear.

Let me explain my theory of fear, my preferences when it comes to terror.

First, I think you need a good laugh once in a while. It makes the terror that much worse.

Second, I think horror and adventure are a perfect mix.

Third, I'm not crazy about buckets of blood. It's easy to fling them around, but it doesn't take much skill, and what you get is as much disgust as true fear. If you're looking for loads of gore, you've come to the wrong place.

I'd rather take you into a long dark hall where you know something horrible is waiting; lead you down that hall, lure you along, so that with every step you want to turn and run, yet find that you can't because you have to go on, to see what happens.

At the end of the hall is a door. And behind that door is a mystery that fills you with dread; something you long for, but fear.

You want to turn. You want to run.

But your hand, almost of its own will, reaches out to open the door....

The lights go out. The door swings open.

And now it's too late to leave. You've entered the first room of the Chamber of Horrors.

The door slams shut.

Welcome to my nightmare.

Bruce Coville

AMULET OF DOOM

PROLOGUE

The castle stood high on a mountain. Its tall windows—arched at the top and so wide an eagle could fly through them without brushing its wingtips—looked out on billowing clouds and valleys that ran deeper than thought.

Inside, Guptas the demon groveled at the feet of the king. Terror twisted the demon's already hideous face into a mask of despair.

"Don't do this to me," he pleaded in a voice that sounded like rough rocks being rubbed together. "I'm not like the others! You know that!"

The king stared at the scaly creature cowering at his feet. "That much is true," he said at last. Contempt and sorrow mingled in his voice. "You are not like the others." He looked away from Guptas. Anger deepened his lonely eyes, and he bent his head in sorrow.

The king was silent for a moment, as if remembering something. A darkness crept across his face, and his features became like stone. "No, Guptas, you are not like the others." He turned back to the demon, and the weariness in his voice seemed as heavy as the mountains surrounding them. "You are far, far worse."

Guptas howled and grasped the king's sandaled foot, cradling it in his scaly claws. Tears hissed from his eyes. Rolling off the king's flesh without effect, they burned into the polished alabaster floor, leaving black pits where they landed.

"It wasn't my fault! *They* made me do it!" The demon's anguished words echoed off the walls of the great chamber. He began to howl, a cry of fear and despair that would have broken the heart of a lesser man.

The king, unmoved, made a noise of contempt in his throat. "You allowed them to 'make' you do it, Guptas. You were weak, and in your weakness you betrayed me. So now you must be punished."

"Don't do this to me!" cried the creature. "Please! I will never betray you again, I swear it!"

"What good is your word?" asked the king wearily. "You are forsworn already. If I had not been alert, I would be dead."

Guptas rolled over and spread his arms and legs, leaving his vulnerable, scaleless belly open to attack. "Kill me!" he screeched. "Kill me now. But don't do this other thing. I beseech you. Have mercy on Guptas who loves you!"

The king turned his face again so that the creature could not see the tear that had formed at the corner of his eye.

Guptas, lost in his own grief, rolled on the floor and jabbered in terror. Suddenly he rose to his knees and flung his arms around the king's legs.

"Remember your son!" he howled, his gravelly voice desperate. "Remember your son!"

The king sighed, and in his voice was the sorrow of a thousand years of loss and pain. "I had *two* sons."

He looked down at Guptas and allowed the mask of his anger to slip for just a moment. "Yes, Guptas. I remember my son. And I remember how you saved his life, though in the long run it did no good. Are you calling on that debt now?"

"Yes!" cried the creature. "Remember how I risked my own life that day! Remember, and be merciful."

"I remember *everything,*" said the king. He turned and walked to his throne. Guptas followed at his heels, sometimes walking, sometimes crawling. His claws scrabbled on the polished stone.

"My judgment is unchanged," said the king.

Guptas raked his claws against his forehead, howling in terror.

"My judgment stands. But this much I will add. When the time is right, I will come for you. I will come, and I will search your heart. And if I feel that I can trust you—"

Guptas threw himself at the king's feet. "You will see!" he cried joyfully. "I can be—"

His words were cut off by a blinding flash of lightning.

Guptas was gone. A jagged scorch mark scarred the

floor where he had stood. A cloud of acrid smoke hung in the air above it.

And the king, the last king in a long line of great kings, and the last man of his race, sat alone in a hall that was large enough to hold a forest and wept.

Day passed into night. At last the king rose from his throne and wandered out of the great hall, into corridors that wound for miles through the empty palace of his fathers.

In his hand he clutched an amulet.

In the center of the amulet was a scarlet stone, still blazing with a fierce heat.

1

ZENOBIA

"Well, I want to tell you, I never smelled anything so awful in my life. The scent of death was just *clinging* to the thing."

Marilyn Sparks paused, a forkful of broccoli halfway to her mouth, and stared at her aunt Zenobia in a combination of awe and astonishment. It was hard to believe any one person could have had so many adventures—and even harder to believe she would dare to tell them at this table.

Marilyn glanced at her father. He was scowling at Zenobia—the same disapproving scowl he used on his English students when they got out of line.

Zenobia ignored him. A fiercely independent woman who had somehow cropped up in a family full of people pleasers, she was long used to scandalizing

5

her relatives. It was almost a tradition, one that had begun way back when she refused to get married and settle down, at a time when living as a single woman was far from fashionable.

That had seemed funny to Marilyn when she first heard it; Zenobia seemed too young to have had such a problem. But then, Marilyn had a hard time remembering that Zenobia Calkins was really her great-aunt and had already seen her seventieth birthday. Marilyn didn't think about age when she thought about Zenobia. She just adored her.

"Anyway," continued Zenobia, "Baron de Courvis drew out his machete and started to hack away at the dead flesh. Of course, in that climate the thing had become a breeding ground for maggots, and—"

Marilyn's mother cut Zenobia off with a sound that was just short of a shriek. "Really, Aunt Zenobia! Couldn't you tell this some other time?"

Marilyn sighed. She should have known she could count on her mother to stop Zenobia right at the most interesting moment. A story about recovering a giant diamond from the intestines of a five-day-dead rogue elephant, no matter how fascinating, simply did not fall within Helen Sparks's definition of table talk. Not even if it came from her father's sister.

Zenobia looked at Mrs. Sparks with something that seemed like pity. "Of course, my dear," she said sweetly. "I don't know what came over me."

Marilyn put the limp broccoli in her mouth and chewed it morosely. Her family was so stodgy!

"You will finish the story later, won't you, Ms. Calkins?" Kyle Patterson, gangly but good-looking, a year older than Marilyn and unfortunately her brother's best friend, had hardly taken a bite since they had sat down to supper. He was much too excited about being at the same table with a great author to eat. It was the first time Marilyn had ever seen Kyle ignore food—and she had known him since he was three.

"I don't know," said Zenobia, with a touch of petulance. "One has to be in the mood for these things to do them properly."

Kyle looked stricken.

"Of course she'll tell us," said Geoff jovially. "Aunt Zenobia never let a good story go untold, did you?"

Marilyn glared at her brother. He was clearly unaware of how deeply their mother had offended Aunt Zenobia.

"Not if the audience is appreciative," agreed Zenobia, deftly skewering a piece of chicken with her fork. "This bird is a trifle bland, by the by," she said sweetly, turning to Marilyn's mother. "You might want to try using a bit of lemon, Helen. They do it that way in Tangiers. It works quite well."

Silence descended on the table.

It is bland, thought Marilyn, hacking a piece from her own serving of PTA-cookbook chicken—a little more savagely than was necessary—and wishing it were some fierce raptor she had somehow managed to kill with her bare hands. *This whole family is bland. Mr. and Mrs. Normal Q. Boring and their children, that's us. I don't know why Kyle bothers with us.*

She looked across the table to where Kyle was sitting, generally oblivious to her presence—as he had been for most of the last fourteen years—and smiled. He had given up on waiting for Zenobia to resume her story and finally started to eat.

7

That's more like it, she thought fondly. *You could use it.*

It wasn't that Kyle was skinny. But he had topped six feet his year, and his body was still filling out to match the growing he had been doing. He had a thatch of tousled blond hair (which Marilyn was itching to brush away from his forehead) and shocking blue eyes that seemed to bore right through her—whenever he bothered to look her way at all. He was at once more silly and more serious than any person she had ever known, and she had no idea why he bothered with her brother, Geoff.

But she was awfully glad he did.

When they gathered together on the porch after supper, Marilyn thought, for a moment, that Kyle had finally noticed her, too. She was leaning against the railing, and he took a place right next to her. She was thrilled, until she realized his reason: It placed him directly across from Zenobia, who was leaning against the opposite railing, next to Geoff. Her parents, of course, were inside—talking about how awful Zenobia was, probably.

Marilyn looked at her aunt and wondered for an instant if Kyle actually found her attractive. She was, after all, a striking woman. Her hair was pure white, really dazzling, so unlike the yellowy gray she saw on other old people. It curled around her face like a billowing cloud, accentuating the depth of her tan. Marilyn knew the time her aunt had spent in the tropical sun had added to her wrinkles. But like everything else about her, the wrinkles were attractive. Every one of them seemed to speak of experience, wisdom, even adventure. They were part of Zenobia. Zenobia was beautiful. So, by definition, the wrinkles were, too.

She was dressed in white cotton—a crisp skirt and a stylish blouse. A sturdy gold chain circled her neck, holding an amulet that—uncharacteristically, and even unstylishly—she kept tucked mysteriously inside her blouse, so that only its upper edge was visible. Marilyn wondered what it looked like. She had a vague recollection that at some time earlier in the evening Zenobia had mentioned that everything she was wearing had come from Egypt.

"So what happened with the diamond, Ms. Calkins?" asked Kyle eagerly.

Zenobia waved her hand. "Oh, the baron cut open the elephant and there it was. We sold it on the coast for a handsome profit."

Kyle looked like someone had pulled his plug. "Is that all?"

"Well, that leaves out the details. But that's how it all came out."

"But it's the details that make it interesting."

"I know that, young man. I have managed to learn a few things in thirty years of writing best-sellers. But it's a little difficult to leap into the middle of a story with both feet. You have to build your momentum. Mine is still in the dining room, under the cake plate."

"I'm sorry about Mom," said Marilyn. "She's pretty set in her ways."

Zenobia dismissed the topic with another wave of her hand. "I've been dealing with the fogeys in this family since I was six years old and shocked them all by announcing I was going to run away with the minister of the Presbyterian church." She paused to reflect for a moment, then added, "Actually, I think I said I was going to *seduce* him, though where I learned that word, I can't remember."

She took out a cigar and bit off the end of it. "That was the beginning of the end, as far as the family was concerned." She struck a wooden match on the porch railing and lit her cigar. She smoked in silence for a moment. The three teenagers waited for her to speak again.

"Maybe I should have stayed in Egypt," she said with a sigh, flicking her ash over the railing. "I got along quite well there. Felt right at home. I always wondered if maybe I had lived there in a previous life."

"Is Cairo as awful as it looks in the movies?" asked Kyle eagerly. He was an old film buff and tended to view the world in terms of what he saw on late-night television.

"Awful? It's wonderful! Did I ever tell you about the time I got caught in a riot there with that fool Eldred Cooley?"

Without waiting for an answer, she launched into a bizarre story involving Egyptian politics, Chinese jewelry, three dancing girls, and a monkey. Kyle settled back contentedly. Marilyn let herself lean ever so slightly in his direction.

It was very pleasant. The evening had an early summer sweetness to it, cool and filled with the scent of fading lilacs and blooming roses. The moon was nearly full, the sky cloudless and smeared with stars. In the background the spring peepers were in full chorus. And Zenobia was at the peak of her form with the bloodcurdling story she was unfolding.

Until the very end, when something strange happened.

"And that was the last I saw of Eldred Cooley!" she said triumphantly. Then her eyes, which had been blazing, seemed to go all cloudy. "The last time but one," she murmured, placing her hand at her throat. Marilyn could hear a troubled note in her voice, and when she looked more closely, she noticed that Zenobia's fingers seemed to tremble as they clasped the golden chain she wore around her neck. Suddenly she tightened her grip. For a moment Marilyn thought she was going to pull off the amulet. "The last time but one," she repeated.

They waited respectfully. But it was almost as if Zenobia had left the porch. Her body was there—her white hair moving lightly in the breeze, her right hand clutching the last inch of her cigar. But she herself seemed to have vanished.

Finally Marilyn could stand the silence no longer. "Aunt Zenobia, are you all right?"

Zenobia blinked. "Of course," she said hurriedly. "I was just thinking about Egypt. Egypt, and Eldred Cooley, and Suleiman."

"You mean Solomon?" asked Kyle eagerly. "Like in *King Solomon's Mines?*"

"No," said Zenobia sharply. "Suleiman, like in Suleiman. A lot of people get them confused. Remind me and I'll tell you about them sometime."

With that she tossed her cigar butt over the porch railing and stalked into the house.

2

THE AMULET

Marilyn, Kyle, and Geoff stood in shocked silence.

"What did I say?" asked Kyle finally.

"Nothing," said Geoff. "Aunt Zenobia's a few strawberries shy of a shortcake is all. You have to expect this kind of thing from her."

"She's not crazy!" snapped Marilyn. "She's brilliant!"

Geoff shrugged. "I didn't say she was stupid. She may have more I.Q. points than all of New Jersey put together. That doesn't mean she could pass the state sanity test. Come on, Kyle—let's go over to your place and shoot a few baskets before we have to turn in."

The two of them banged down the steps, leaving Marilyn alone on the porch. She twisted a lock of her red hair in tight circles around her finger. She would never admit it to Geoff, but there *was* something strange going on with Aunt Zenobia. She had been oddly distracted ever since she arrived—sometimes seeming like her old self, other times drifting off into a kind of trance, as she had just now. A couple of times Marilyn had caught her fingering the chain of that amulet and staring blankly into space.

Marilyn had mentioned it to her mother last night, but Mrs. Sparks claimed it was just prepublication jitters. "After all, Aunt Zenobia's new book is scheduled to be released in two weeks. It's natural for her to be a bit nervous about what the critics will say. Especially," she had added maliciously, "if it's as weird as the last one. Honestly, I don't know where that woman gets her ideas."

At least Aunt Zenobia has *ideas,* Marilyn had thought unkindly.

She began to dawdle her way down the porch steps. Moving dreamily, she trailed her fingers along the railing, still thinking about Zenobia. When she reached the flagstone walk that led to the street, Brick came wandering up to rub against her legs.

Brick was the Sparkses' cat, a black-and-white stray they had taken in a few years ago. After three weeks of trying to name him, they had settled on Brick, because her father claimed that was exactly what the cat was as dumb as.

Now Brick was meowing for attention. So Marilyn scooped him up. Then she turned to look at the house.

It was an old place, built sometime around the turn of the century. She was glad of that. Occasionally she thought she might like to live in one of the more modern houses that had sprung up lately on the outskirts of town. But every time she spent the night with one of her girlfriends, she realized how much she would miss the creaky old place she had called home for so long. There was something different about a house that had been lived in—a sense of ongoing life, a kind of old-shoe comfort that she never felt in a newer place.

"Isn't that right, Brick?" she asked the cat, as if he could read her mind.

Brick looked at her as if he couldn't believe his ears. Then he reached out a paw and batted her on the side of the face.

"Be that way," she said, dropping him unceremoniously to the ground. He meowed in protest and began rubbing about her legs to be picked back up.

She ignored him and turned her thoughts back to the house. The fact that the place really belonged to Zenobia, that she had lived here as a girl herself, made it even more special. Her ownership was also the reason that Marilyn's parents, even though they paid a respectable rent, could hardly refuse Zenobia whenever she decided to visit. Marilyn was glad of that. Given their own way, they would probably have tried to find some excuse to make the old woman stay at the Kennituck Falls Motel.

She tried to imagine life without Zenobia. The prospect was so dull it made her shudder.

She heard the thump of a basketball on asphalt coming from Kyle's driveway, and the excited shouts of her brother and his friend. The sounds made her feel lonely. Rubbing her arms against the cool of the breeze, which was starting to pick up strength, she hurried back to the house.

Brick, still feeling affectionate, followed at her heels.

In her room she stripped off her jeans and blouse and burrowed into an old flannel nightgown. The pink plaid fabric was far from glamorous, but it did have the virtues of being warm, soft, and exceedingly comfortable.

Marilyn popped the cast album from *Carousel*, her favorite Broadway show, into the CD player, then flopped across her bed and tried to figure out her aunt's curious behavior on the porch. Brick curled up on her back and began to rumble his deep, familiar purr.

After a round of intense but unproductive thought Marilyn decided to chalk Zenobia's mood up to the peculiarities that accompany genius, forget it, and go to sleep.

Hours later she was still wide awake. She tossed and turned, practiced deep breathing, and even tried counting sheep. It was no use. Sleep would not come.

She was not used to being awake at this time of night. Usually she dropped right off.

She sat up in bed. The silence was driving her out of her mind.

Heaving a sigh, she went to her dresser and picked up her brush. She looked in the mirror and grimaced as she began to work the brush through her tangles. Anyone named Sparks should be spared the burden of having such bright red hair.

Well, she thought as she began the vigorous brushing, *at least I was spared the freckles.*

Somewhere after the thirtieth stroke she heard a knock at her door.

Marilyn paused, the brush still in her hair. She glanced at the clock on her nightstand.

It was after two.

"Who is it?" she asked softly.

The door opened a crack; Zenobia peered into the room. A smile creased her face. "Thank goodness you're still awake. I have to talk to you!"

Marilyn put down her brush and crossed to the door. "Come in," she said, swinging it open. She was delighted to see her aunt. But she was also very confused—and a little frightened. Because in Zenobia's eye she had caught a glimpse, brief but unmistakable, of something she had never expected to see there.

She had caught a glimpse of fear.

And the idea of something that could make Zenobia Calkins afraid sent shivers trembling up and down Marilyn's spine.

A moment later Zenobia was sitting cross-legged on Marilyn's bed. She wore a loose-fitting cotton gown and a white linen robe. Except for her white hair, now hanging loose and long over her shoulders, from behind she would have looked like any of a dozen of Marilyn's friends who had sat in the same position while they held forth on life, religion, and the meaning of boys.

Marilyn sat quietly, waiting for her aunt to tell her what was on her mind.

"Egypt is very old," said Zenobia at last.

Marilyn nodded, uncertain of how to respond to such a comment.

"It is filled with strange things," added Zenobia after a another long silence. "Ancient things. Things that perhaps should not be disturbed."

Marilyn remained silent.

"I'm boring you," said Zenobia.

"No!" exclaimed Marilyn. "I just don't know what to say."

"How could you," muttered Zenobia. "I'm rambling like ... like an old woman!" She laughed—a dry, harsh sound. "I'm sorry I bothered you. I had a nightmare, and I wanted to talk to someone."

Marilyn nodded. She knew what it was like to wake up in the middle of the night with terror ripping at your heart. She supposed even the bravest people in the world had nightmares. "Tell me about it."

Zenobia shook her head. "I don't think I want to."

"Then tell me about Egypt. Tell me about Solomon and Suleiman, like you said you would."

Zenobia looked at her suspiciously. "Why do you want to know about that?"

"Because I love your stories," replied Marilyn truthfully.

Zenobia nodded. "Solomon and Suleiman," she said. "History and myth. Reality and magic."

She had a faraway look in her eyes, the same look Marilyn had seen when they were on the porch.

"The thing is, people get them confused," said Zenobia. "Solomon and Suleiman, that is. They're not the same person, as a lot of people seem to believe."

Marilyn, who had never heard of Suleiman, and only remembered Solomon vaguely from some long-forgotten sermon, nodded wisely.

"Solomon came later," said Zenobia. "He's the one

you'll find in the Bible—Solomon's Temple, Solomon and Sheba, and so on. The Koran says he had power over the winds; he would put his throne on a huge carpet made of green silk, and he and his army could fly all over the world that way. The jinn were supposed to be at his command."

"Jinn?"

"Genies," explained Zenobia. "At least, that's how you've probably heard of them. I suppose all that might have been so. But I doubt it. Magic was well on the way out by that time anyway."

"You talk as if magic was real once."

Zenobia shrugged. "Who's to say? When you've traveled in as many places as I have, wild places, primitive places, you see things that can't really be explained. Is it magic? I don't know. It might be. But not great magic. The great magic is all gone."

"Why did you want to tell me about Solomon?" asked Marilyn.

"I didn't. You asked."

"But you mentioned him on the porch," persisted Marilyn. "Egypt, and Eldred Cooley, and Solomon. Or was it Suleiman?" She shook her head in frustration. "Now I'm totally confused!"

"It was Suleiman," said Zenobia at last. "Egypt, and Eldred Cooley, and Suleiman. Egypt is the most important place in the world, at least to me. Eldred Cooley was a friend. Not a particularly good friend, but the most interesting one I ever had. He died late last year."

She shivered, and Marilyn sensed a story, another story hidden behind the one she was being told. She wanted to interrupt, but Zenobia had started again.

"Suleiman made this amulet, which Eldred gave me shortly before his death. It has nothing to do with Egypt, other than the fact that Eldred found it there. How it got to Egypt I have no idea."

As she was talking, Zenobia pulled the amulet from her nightgown.

Marilyn caught her breath. It was unbelievably beautiful.

Zenobia stared down at it for a long time. "Take it," she said at last. "I want you to keep it for me." As she spoke she began to draw the golden chain over her head.

"I can't do that. It's too precious! Besides, it's yours. Your friend gave it to you."

Zenobia snorted. "What sort of a friend do you suppose he was, giving me this?" Suddenly she reached forward and grabbed Marilyn by the wrists, her grip so hard it was almost painful. "I'm *not* giving it to you," she added fiercely. "That's important for you to know. I just want you to guard it for me."

"Aunt Zenobia, you're hurting me," whispered Marilyn.

Zenobia looked startled and released her hold on Marilyn's wrists. Marilyn shivered. It wasn't the strength of her aunt's grip that frightened her so much as it was the look in her eyes—the same look they had held when Zenobia first entered her room; the look of fear.

"I'm sorry," said Zenobia hoarsely. "Please—take the amulet and keep it safe until I can figure out what to do about it."

Though her voice was neutral, her eyes were filled

with desperation. They pleaded with Marilyn, and there was no way she could refuse her aunt's request.

"All right," she said, her voice reluctant. "I'll take care of it for you."

"Thank you," whispered Zenobia. "Thank you, Marilyn. I'll pay you back, somehow. I promise."

Then she rose from the bed and hurried out of the room before Marilyn had a chance to ask any of the dozen questions vying with one another in her mind.

"Wait!" she called, reaching out anxiously. It was too late. The door swung shut, and Zenobia was gone.

Marilyn sat for a long time, staring at the amulet. It was made of a polished blue stone she couldn't identify. Set in its center was a blood-red gem.

She cupped the amulet in her hand, staring at it curiously. It was wonderful to hold something so beautiful, and she felt a surge of possessiveness rising in her, a feeling that she never wanted to give it back.

But when she extended her finger to touch the sparkling scarlet jewel, she cried out and drew back her finger in surprise. The jewel was hot, so hot that it hurt to touch it.

Even stranger, it sent a tingle like electricity racing up her arm.

3
NIGHTMARE

"**M**arilyn! Hey, Marilyn, wake up. Class is over!"

Seeing that the words failed to rouse Marilyn from her trancelike state, Alicia Graves, a short girl with spiky blond hair, gave her a jab on her upper arm and shouted, "Hey, Sparks! Red alert! The aliens have landed and we need every able-bodied woman to keep them from carrying off our men!"

Marilyn came out of her trance with a jolt, knocking three pens and a pencil to the floor.

"Nice work, Airhead," said Alicia sardonically. At the same time she bent to pick up the items Marilyn had knocked over.

Marilyn rubbed her hands over her face. "Sorry, Licorice. I'm kind of out of it today."

Marilyn had been dubbed "Airhead" and Alicia "Licorice" eight years ago, on the first day of third grade, which was when the two girls had first met. The names had been given during a playground squabble. They had patched it up the next morning and been best friends ever since.

"It's all right," said Alicia, depositing the pens on Marilyn's desk. "I suppose it's not easy being a dip. I'll keep the pencil, though. I could use one."

"Spoken like a true dwarf," said Marilyn, tucking the pens out of Alicia's reach, in case she should decide she also needed one of those.

"Hey, short people got rights," said Alicia, drawing herself up to her full five feet one and three-quarter inches.

"That's true," said Marilyn. "They got rights, and they got lefts. They also got tops and bottoms. What they don't got is much in the middle."

"You die, flame-brain," said Alicia, who had (much to Marilyn's astonishment) long envied Marilyn's bright red hair. "But not until you tell me why you're doing such a good imitation of the walking dead today."

Marilyn shrugged. "I didn't get much sleep last night." That was true, as far as it went, though it didn't say much about why.

Alicia knew her friend well enough to make a good guess anyway. "Whassa matter? That crazy aunt of yours keep you up all night telling stories?"

"She's not crazy!"

"Well, she ain't normal."

"Who is? Come on, we'll be late for gym."

* * *

As it turned out, they were late for gym anyway. Marilyn, half-undressed in front of her locker, fell into a trance and was still standing there when Alicia came back from delivering a note her doctor had sent to the instructor.

"Oh, give me a break," she sputtered when she saw Marilyn staring into space. "What is it with you today, Sparks?"

Marilyn looked down at her half-dressed body and shook her head. "Just showing off, I guess," she said, forcing a laugh.

"Save it for someone who can appreciate it. Me, I'd rather go stare at the wrestling team. Finish getting ready before we both get in trouble."

Marilyn changed in silence. But her mind was racing. Her aunt's strange behavior, and the mysterious amulet, had been dominating her thoughts all day, making it impossible to concentrate on anything else. Her thoughts kept drifting back to the conversation in her bedroom, and the fear in Zenobia's eyes.

Part of her wanted to tell Alicia about the conversation—and the amulet. But she knew her friend would merely claim it was her famous imagination at work and tell her to wise up. Another part resisted telling her anyway. Especially about the amulet. That just felt like a wonderful secret that she wanted to keep to herself.

But if she couldn't start concentrating on something else, she was going to end up in big trouble before the day was over. Teachers at Burton-Speake High were not partial to daydreamers.

"I know what it is!" shouted Alicia, interrupting her thoughts. "You're cooking up some lamebrained scheme to go off with your aunt when she leaves on her next trip. Well, cool your imagination, Airhead. Let's head for the gym before we get in more trouble than we're in already."

Marilyn closed her locker and followed her friend's stocky form out of the room. *Cool your imagination!* indeed. Alicia must be really fed up with her daydreaming today or she would never have said that. She knew very well how tired Marilyn was of people telling her not to let her imagination run away with her.

Despite her indignation, Marilyn did try to concentrate on gym class. She wasn't very successful, though, and ended up being hit twice with the volleyball because she was too absorbed in her own thoughts to pay attention to the game.

"You ought to go out for the Olympics," said Alicia as they left the locker room after class.

Marilyn was working on a suitable retort when the lanky figure of Kyle Patterson ambled around the corner. His shirt, as usual, was only half tucked in. "Hey," he said cheerfully. "It's Sparky Junior!"

Marilyn considered punching him. Her brother, not surprisingly, was known as Sparky to all his friends. Equally unsurprising was the fact that about half of them referred to her as Sparky Junior. Even so, the words always activated a primitive instinct deep inside her: namely, the urge to kill.

Even when it came from Kyle.

"What do you want, Lurch?" snarled Alicia. Unlike Marilyn, she was not very fond of Kyle.

"Bug off, fireplug. I'm talking to your friend."

Alicia grumbled something about biting him on the

knee. Marilyn, doing her best to forget "Sparky Junior," smiled sweetly and asked Kyle what he wanted.

"I was just wondering if your aunt told you any more about King Solomon last night." He leaned against a locker. "You're really lucky, you know. Having someone like that for an aunt. She's fantastic."

"I know," said Marilyn. She hesitated for a moment, then said, "Why don't you have supper with us again tonight? I'm sure my mother wouldn't mind. Then you can ask Aunt Zenobia about Solomon yourself."

"Do you think that would be okay?"

Alicia snorted. "Are you kidding? You eat over there so often now her father could claim you as a dependent on his taxes."

"Yeah, but he'd probably rather have you," retorted Kyle. "Then he could use the short form." Turning to Marilyn, he said, "Thanks for the invite. I'll see you tonight."

He walked away too quickly for Alicia to think of a comeback to his short joke. Marilyn watched him go, a dreamy expression on her face.

"I don't know what you see in that jerk," growled Alicia.

Marilyn laughed. "He's adorable!"

"So are teddy bears . . . and *they* keep their mouths shut!"

Supper was a disaster. Instead of being fascinating and witty, Zenobia was cranky and out of sorts. Marilyn had never seen her aunt this way before, and she wondered if she was ill.

Kyle, sitting next to Zenobia, tried desperately to draw her into telling a story until finally she snapped at him. He withdrew like a whipped puppy for the rest of the meal, and Marilyn wanted nothing so much as to reach out and cuddle him and make him feel better.

As soon as they could politely manage it, Kyle and Geoff excused themselves and went off to shoot baskets, leaving Marilyn alone with Zenobia and her parents. After a while Marilyn headed for her room, preferring isolation to the tension that hung over the living room.

She sat on her bed, staring at the amulet, which she had taken from her dresser drawer. It had occupied her thoughts all day anyway. The funny thing was, now that she could really examine it, she didn't know what she was looking for.

Brick sprawled on her lap, purring loudly. Every once in a while he would bat lazily at the amulet, making it twist on the end of the golden chain. The first time he struck at it, Marilyn feared he would get a shock, as she had the night before. When he didn't seem to feel anything, she gathered her courage and touched the jewel again. She was almost disappointed to find that it felt completely normal.

She heard voices downstairs and wondered what was going on. In her usual imaginative fashion she pictured a dreadful fight between Zenobia and her parents. The talking stopped. She was still trying to imagine her aunt's triumphant final remark—her imagination was wild, but not wild enough to conceive of her parents winning an encounter with Zenobia—when someone tapped on her door.

Brick sprang up and bounded off her lap.

"Idiot," said Marilyn fondly. Then she called, "Come in!"

It was Zenobia. When she saw the amulet in Marilyn's fingers, she smiled in relief.

"I just wanted to make sure nothing had happened to it," she said. Crossing to the bed, she sat down and took the amulet from Marilyn, letting it dangle from her fingers. The soft burnish of the gold chain gleamed dully in the lamplight. The red jewel winked and sparkled. "Pretty, isn't it?" she whispered.

Marilyn reached for the amulet, and Zenobia dropped it into her hand. She held it up, letting it dangle between them like an unanswered question. "It's beautiful," she agreed. "But it makes me nervous."

Zenobia raised an eyebrow.

"It's that stone in the center," said Marilyn, feeling silly. "It's almost like an eye." She shrugged. "I'm being foolish, I suppose."

"Not really," said Zenobia.

Marilyn started to tell her aunt about the amulet shocking her the night before, but couldn't bring herself to say the words. It just seemed too ridiculous. In fact, she was beginning to wonder if she had imagined it.

"Why do you want me to keep it, anyway?" she asked. "What could possibly happen to it here in Kennituck Falls?"

Zenobia pushed at Marilyn's hand. "It's just safer with you right now, that's all." She turned to the corner where Brick was lurking and made a little noise with her tongue.

Marilyn was astonished to see the cat, who usually hated strangers, come bounding over to her.

"Cats are very important," said Zenobia, scratching Brick behind his ears. "Take good care of him."

"I do. But you didn't really answer my question."

Zenobia sighed. "You make me feel like a hypocrite."

Marilyn blinked in surprise.

"Listen," said the old woman. "I've never been one to believe that ignorance is bliss. And I'm certainly the last who can advise against curiosity. But in this case—well, I think the less you know the better."

"Thanks a lot!"

Zenobia laughed. "You're too much like me for your own good. I'll tell you what. Once I solve this mess, I'll tell you the whole story. Will that be a fair trade for my silence now?"

"I guess so," said Marilyn reluctantly.

"Good. Now, why don't you put the thing away. You look like you could use a decent night's sleep."

She rose from the bed and left the room as quickly as she had entered.

Brick yowled as Zenobia closed the door behind her, sounding as though he had just lost his best friend.

Marilyn sighed and tucked the amulet under her pillow.

A few minutes later she was asleep.

* * *

The dream started innocently enough. She and Kyle were bicycling down a country lane, with a picnic lunch stowed in their backpacks.

She was wearing the amulet around her neck.

They found a beautiful tree-shaded spot beside a little stream and settled down to have lunch. The day was warm and sunny, the air sweet and clean. But suddenly everything went dark.

"Give me the amulet!" said a hoarse voice.

"I can't!" Marilyn cried. "It's not mine. It belongs to my aunt!"

"No, it doesn't," said the voice. "It belongs to *me*."

The sun had disappeared completely. The air was cold and smelled of something terrible and unclean. She leaned against Kyle, but he felt funny. She turned to look at him, and his face began to change, change into something horrible.

"The amulet!" he said, and his voice was the same voice that had come out of nowhere a moment earlier. "Give me the amulet!"

"No!' she screamed. "I can't!"

She tried to draw away from him, but his arms were tight about her, hot and scaly and smelling of death. She beat at his chest and her hands sank right into it.

They burned.

"The amulet," he said again. His eyes were pits of fire now, his nose an upturned horror with ragged nostrils in the middle of his scaly face. He opened his mouth and a forked tongue flickered between yellow fangs. "Give me the amulet!"

When she refused, he lowered his head toward her

neck. She could feel hot breath, and the drip of burning saliva. . . .

Marilyn sat up, her body covered with a cold sweat. Brick stood hissing at the end of the bed, back arched and fur raised as though he had just spotted a dog.

Marilyn fought back tears. "It was only a dream," she whispered. "Only a dream."

Then, prompted by a suspicion she couldn't explain, she thrust her hand under the pillow.

The amulet was gone.

4

THE TOUCH OF

DEATH

Marilyn sat in the small pool of light cast by her bed lamp, body rigid with fright.

Zenobia, she thought, when the fear released its grip on her brain enough for her to think at all. *I've got to get Aunt Zenobia.*

Yet for a moment she was unable to climb out of bed. The nightmare was too fresh in her memory, the fear too strong. The bed itself seemed like the only island of safety in a dark world of hidden horrors.

Brick jumped to the floor. The thump of his landing sent her heart leaping into her throat, and she let out a gasp of fear. The cat looked up at her. She could have sworn he was afraid, too. She cursed herself for being overimaginative.

Overimaginative or not, the amulet was gone. She had been trusted with it, and now it was missing.

Taking a deep breath, she climbed out of her bed. But when she reached the door, she stopped. Before she went to get Zenobia, she should make sure the thing was really missing. She'd look like a real jerk rousing her aunt and then finding that the amulet had only slipped to the floor while she was sleeping.

She shook herself and smiled. Of course that was what had happened! The amulet was still under her pillow, just in a slightly different place. That nightmare must have really rattled her brains, for her to panic this way.

Though it was a wonderful solution, unfortunately it turned out to be wrong. When Marilyn returned to her bed and pulled aside her pillow, she found nothing but an expanse of white linen.

Frantic again, she dropped to the floor and reached under her bed, hoping perhaps the amulet had slid over the top of the mattress and landed among the dust kitties.

As she groped in the darkness she felt something grab her hand. Her heart, already in her throat and with no place left to go, seemed to stop for a moment. Then she felt the familiar jab of a sharp little tooth and crumpled against the bed in relief.

"Brick! Get out of there, you idiot!"

She dragged the cat, who went limp in protest, from under the bed. Then she lifted the edge of the sheet and looked into the darkness where he had been lurking.

The bed lamp wasn't bright enough. She needed more light.

Sliding open the drawer in her nightstand, she fumbled around for the little flashlight she kept there. It was a habit she had developed more than ten years ago, to help her through her occasional bouts of fear of the dark. They didn't come often, but when they did they were overwhelming.

Right now she was too worried about the missing amulet to be afraid. She simply needed the flashlight to see better.

Lying flat on her stomach, she cast its beam under her bed and looked anxiously for the dull gleam of gold.

She saw three socks and a great deal of dust, but no amulet.

Cursing to herself, she got back to her knees. She looked at the bed. Maybe the amulet had gotten caught in the sheets, or between the top of the mattress and the headboard.

Five minutes later the bed had been stripped to the mattress pad, and the mattress itself pulled a half foot back from the headboard.

The amulet was nowhere to be found.

Which left her right back where she had started. She had to get Zenobia.

Marilyn hesitated. How could she tell her aunt she had lost the amulet?

"But I didn't lose it," she protested out loud, causing Brick, who had been playing in the pile of sheets, to skittle under a chair. "I *couldn't* have lost it. It was there when I went to sleep."

That was when she realized that the alternative was just as bad: If she hadn't lost it, someone must have taken it. Someone had come into her room while she slept, reached under her pillow, and stolen the amulet.

She shivered, thinking of what else the unknown thief could have done.

But who was it? Who besides Zenobia even knew she had the thing?

She had to get her aunt.

Marilyn took a moment to brace herself. She was not looking forward to breaking the news to Zenobia. Finally she took a deep breath and headed into the hallway. She had her flashlight in one hand, and Brick tucked under her arm. She was taking the cat along for comfort. She would have preferred to have taken him for *protection*, but she was well aware he would be useless in any kind of emergency.

The floor was cold. She wished she had thought to put on slippers.

The silence seemed to beat at her. It was the silence of an old house, filled with memories, filled with the days and nights of the people who had lived here, a silence that was not quite silence, and not quite safe. At least, that was how it seemed to Marilyn in her overwrought condition.

She reached Zenobia's door and knocked softly, then waited, shifting nervously from one foot to the other.

No answer.

She knocked again.

Still no answer.

"Aunt Zenobia?"

She knocked a third time, more loudly still, then dropped Brick to the floor and gently turned the knob.

The cat let out a bloodcurdling yowl and disappeared down the hallway. Marilyn jumped, almost dropping the flashlight, and cursed under her breath.

"Aunt Zenobia!" she hissed. "It's me—Marilyn. I have to talk to you."

Still no answer. She pushed the door open a little farther and shone her light into the room. The feeble beam fell on something that gleamed a dull yellow—a golden chain. Shifting the flashlight just slightly, she felt relief surge through her. The amulet was dangling from Zenobia's fingers, its great central jewel sparkling in the beam of the flashlight. Zenobia must have come into her room while she slept and retrieved the thing.

But why?

"Aunt Zenobia?"

She stepped into the room, overcome with curiosity. Her aunt had been willing to wake her the night before. Surely she would not complain if Marilyn did the same thing now.

"Aunt Zenobia!" she said more loudly. At the same time she moved the beam of her flashlight up the bed.

It clattered to the floor, and she clasped her hands over her mouth as a wave of cold horror flooded her body. She felt herself sway. Afraid she was going to faint, she dropped to her knees and leaned forward, resting her forehead against the floor.

For a long time she could not force herself to move.

That Zenobia was dead there was no question. But Marilyn had seen dead people before. The sight, while unpleasant, was not enough to drive her to her knees.

Part of what was hitting her so hard right now was shock, of course. But beyond that, and far more appalling than death itself, was the rictus of fear that had contorted Zenobia's face in her last moments. It was her open, staring eyes and what could only be a scream of horror frozen on her face that made Marilyn's insides churn.

How long she stayed that way, her body quaking, her head pressed against the floor, she could not have said.

What finally forced her to move was the tiniest bit of doubt. What if her aunt was not dead? What if she had had a heart attack and was still alive, just barely, needing help, needing someone . . .

Marilyn forced herself to raise her head from the floor. Zenobia's arm, dangling over the edge of the bed, the golden chain of the amulet tangled in her fingers, was close enough to touch.

Slowly she reached forward.

The flesh of the wrist was still warm.

But there was not the slightest sign of a pulse.

Marilyn was silent for a moment, grief engulfing her. She couldn't bear to look at her aunt. But the image of that contorted face, glimpsed during one brief instant of horror, still burned in her mind.

She leaned her face against Zenobia's hand and wept.

Her tears fell on the amulet. When they touched it, a rough voice, seeming to come from nowhere, growled, "Give that amulet to me!"

Then, even more terrifying, Marilyn felt her aunt's fingers tighten around the mysterious ornament. At the same time she sensed power in the room, a crackle that was almost electric.

As suddenly as it had come, it vanished. For a moment Zenobia's hand, soft and smelling of spice, rested itself against her cheek.

And then Zenobia's voice, kind and calm, spoke in

her mind: *Be brave, Marilyn. Be brave, because I am going to need your help.*

The joy Marilyn felt at hearing her aunt's voice vanished with her next words, for even after death Zenobia's voice quivered with horror when she spoke them.

Be careful, Marilyn. Be careful . . . and beware of Guptas!

The hand went limp. Zenobia's presence vanished.

As if a spell had been broken, Marilyn's voice returned, and she began to scream.

5

A LETTER FROM
ZENOBIA

Marilyn sat in the kitchen, drinking a cup of hot chocolate. She had a dark blue blanket wrapped around her shoulders. Her mother stood behind her, rubbing her neck.

Upstairs they could hear the men from the ambulance service poking around in Zenobia's room.

"Why were you in there, anyway?" asked Mrs. Sparks softly.

Marilyn sighed. She had already answered the question twice. Wearily she told about the missing amulet for the third time. "I was worried about it, because I figured it was very valuable. And I thought Aunt Zenobia might still be awake. Sometimes she writes . . ." she stopped, corrected herself. "She used to write in the middle of the night, sometimes."

"I know," said Mrs. Sparks. Her voice carried the old note of disapproval. "She used to keep me awake."

Let it rest! thought Marilyn. *The woman is dead. Can't you finally stop resenting her?*

Her father appeared at the doorway. "Well, they're gone," he said. He walked to the table and dropped heavily into one of the creaky chairs.

Geoff came in after him, looking glum. He had not been nearly as fond of Zenobia as Marilyn was. Even so, her death had struck him deeply.

"What happens now?" asked Marilyn. Her voice had a tiny quaver in it.

"They'll take her to Flannigan's," said Mr. Sparks wearily, as if he knew the routine all too well. "She'll be embalmed. Tomorrow we'll go and pick out a coffin. There'll be viewing hours. Relatives we haven't seen in years will show up, expecting to be fed and sheltered."

"Don't be cynical, Harvey," said Mrs. Sparks. "There'll be plenty of people *bringing* food."

"Don't forget the reporters," said Geoff.

Mrs. Sparks looked startled. "What?"

"Reporters," repeated Geoff. "Aunt Zenobia was famous. Plus she had that new book coming out next month. Her publisher was pushing it as her best ever. This is going to be big news."

"Oh, God," moaned his mother. "I hadn't thought of that."

"Will they be able to fix her face?" asked Marilyn suddenly.

"What?"

"Her face," she repeated impatiently. "It looked awful. Will they be able to fix it?"

Mr. Sparks actually chuckled. "Of course they will, sweetheart. It's not that unusual to have facial contortions with a heart attack. They'll just—"

"I don't want to know how!" said Marilyn vehemently. "I just wanted to make sure they could do it. Aunt Zenobia was beautiful and people should remember her that way."

They sat for another hour, talking quietly in the way that people do when the presence of death has been brought to their minds. The night was still dark when they made their way back to their separate rooms, their separate fears.

It's funny how death enters a house, Marilyn thought, lying in her bed. *It comes to steal the most precious thing of all, and it doesn't make any difference how many locks you have on the doors. When it wants to come in, it comes in.*

She had often wondered if death was accidental or planned. Was there a time when you were destined to die, a time that nothing could change, one way or the other? Or was death just something that happened, willy-nilly, with no rhyme or reason?

She sighed in annoyance, then turned and fluffed her pillow. Those kinds of thoughts confused her. She dropped her head back onto the pillow and drew the covers up around her.

Brick jumped onto the bed and began kneading his paws against the comforter.

Marilyn was glad to have his company. After all that had happened, she didn't want to be alone. Lulled by the low rumble of the cat's purr, she began to drift toward sleep. But as she did, her rebellious mind began to replay the horror of finding Zenobia's corpse, and all the strange things that had happened in her aunt's room.

After several minutes of tossing and turning, Marilyn sat up and looked around her familiar room. Every shadow seemed filled with danger. She pulled Brick to her chest and held him close.

What am I going to do? she wondered. *Aunt Zenobia wants me to be brave. But right now I'm scared out of my mind.*

She thought, briefly, about telling her mother about the things she had heard in Aunt Zenobia's room. But she had been chastised too many times for her "wild imaginings" to think she would get any sympathy for this story.

No, for now she was on her own.

Unless you counted Aunt Zenobia.

To Marilyn's enormous relief her parents didn't force her to go to school. Unfond as they had been of Zenobia themselves, they recognized their daughter's grief and allowed her to stay home to deal with it.

She spent the morning helping her mother make a list of relatives who had to be called. Later they went through Zenobia's clothing and picked out the outfit she would be buried in. The idea startled Marilyn; it had never before occurred to her that someone actually had to do these things.

After lunch she accompanied her father to Flannigan's and helped him choose an elaborate mahogany coffin. That had pleased Marilyn. She thought the coffin was beautiful, and that Zenobia would have liked it.

Somewhere in her mind she was vaguely aware of her father's concern about Zenobia's will. The house they lived in had been hers, after all, and now it would belong to someone else. Possibly them, possibly not. Even Marilyn had to admit that her beloved aunt had been eccentric enough that she might have left the place to anyone. It could well turn out that they had to move.

She shoved the thought to the back of her mind. It was too much to deal with right now.

So the day was sad, but bearable. Things didn't turn terrifying until the middle of that night, when Marilyn woke to find Brick lying on her chest.

When she stirred, the big cat opened his eyes. They were blazing red.

Then he spoke.

"Get the amulet!"

His voice sounded like two rough stones rubbing together.

Marilyn screamed and flung the cat from the bed. He yowled once, a sharp, horrifying sound. Then, looking oddly empty, he crouched by the baseboard, staring pathetically up at her.

Marilyn buried her face in her pillow and began to cry.

What was going on here?

An hour later, when the light began to creep over the edge of her window, she wondered if the incident with Brick had been a dream.

The last twenty-four hours had been like a dream

anyway, a period she had moved through like a mario-
nette, walking, talking, but all the time feeling as
though someone else were pulling her strings. The
feeling came not because she felt she was being forced
to do things she didn't want to, but simply because
she felt too weak to do anything on her own.

She heard Geoff singing in the shower and heaved
herself out of bed. Knowing her parents, it was un-
likely she would be allowed another day off from
school.

She looked around. Brick was nowhere to be seen.

She shivered. Had he really talked to her?

Or was she just losing her mind?

She threw on her robe and went to pound on the
bathroom door. Geoff would stay wet and off-key forever if she didn't.

"Be out in a minute!" he yelled, which meant she
could expect him in ten.

Walking back toward her room, she stopped, almost
against her will, beside Zenobia's door.

A thrill of horror tingled through her. In the morning light the rational part of her mind dismissed what
had happened in Zenobia's room two nights ago as a
figment of her overwrought imagination. Common
sense told her there had been no voices, no touch
from the dead woman's hand.

Another part of her, more daring, clung to the
memory and insisted it was reality.

"I'm going to need your help," the voice had
whispered.

The words had been repeating in her mind ever
since. What kind of help could a dead person need?

Marilyn blinked. She had stepped into Zenobia's room without realizing what she was doing.

She looked around. Her mother had had no time to come in here and clean things out. Other than a change of sheets, the place looked pretty much as it had the night of Zenobia's death.

For a moment Marilyn felt like an intruder. Then she decided she was glad to be here, because it made her feel closer to Zenobia.

She had crossed to the dresser and was examining her aunt's bottles of perfume (several) and her selection of cosmetics (minimal) when she spotted an envelope sticking out from under the dresser scarf. Pulling it out, she felt a little tingle run down her spine.

It was addressed to her.

Fingers trembling, she opened it.

Dear Marilyn,

I have just left your room, and I suddenly find myself doubting whether I should have asked you to guard the amulet for me after all. I am feeling very guilty about it.

The rational part of my mind says I am just being foolish. But another part says I may have done a terrible thing.

If I have, I hope Heaven, and you, will forgive me.

I'm afraid, Marilyn. I think I am in great danger. It may seem silly, but if anything should happen to me, there are some things you should know about the amulet.

I had the thing, as you may remember, from my "friend" Eldred Cooley, who was a second-rate archaeologist with first-rate ambitions. Eldred found it in the Egyptian desert several years ago. He showed it to me then, with the declaration that there was something "special" about it that he was going to figure out.

It seems perhaps he did. Last year I ran into Eldred again in Cairo and we went to dinner. After he had a little too much to drink, he began to talk more freely than he should have.

He told me he had discovered the secret of the amulet and that within a month he would be rich beyond his wildest dreams.

When I expressed my skepticism he rattled on with a wild story about an ancient race of giants who had created a great civilization while mankind was still grubbing for subsistence in primitive villages. He called them the Suleimans and claimed they were the basis for any number of myths and religious beliefs throughout the East. He said the amulet was an artifact of their culture.

He must have seen the disbelief in my face, because he got angry and said he would prove it to me. I ignored his comments as the ravings of a drunk—until later that night when he showed up at the door of my hotel room.

He was holding an exquisite metal box engraved with strange markings.

And he was dying.

I took one look at him and dragged him through the door. He was gasping for breath. His skin was mottled with blotches of black and purple, and his hands were horribly swollen.

"Look at this, Zenobia," he whispered, holding

out the box. "Then tell me if you still think I'm crazy."

Ignoring the box, I threw him onto the couch and tore open his shirt collar. It did no good. His neck was so swollen his air pipes were being crushed.

I ran to the phone to call a doctor.

"Don't!" he whispered. "It's too late. And I have to talk to you. I have to tell you something."

I knelt by his side and cradled his head in my arms. I had to struggle to keep from vomiting; a terrible stench rose from his body. My nausea grew when he reached for my hand with his swollen, discolored fingers.

"The amulet," he whispered, holding it out to me with his other hand. "I want you to have the amulet." He smiled. It was pathetic. "I always wanted to give you something special, Zenobia. Here it is."

He began to cough, only his throat was so swollen the air could not get out, and he shook with agony.

"Great power here," he whispered. "But you must be careful. Be careful, Zenobia." He tried to cough again. His fingers tightened on mine. "Be careful. And don't trust Guptas!"

"What do you mean?" I asked.

It was too late. He was dead.

The details of what happened next—the police, the government, the doctors—aren't important, though you should know about the box.

Marilyn, that box was an unbelievable find. I know some archaeology, and the condition, the workmanship, the age of this piece made it the kind of discovery an archaeologist would kill for.

The Egyptian government has it now, and they're not talking about it.

As for myself, I have not spent a peaceful night since then. I have been tormented by the most horrible nightmares, and . . .

Well, I think I made a foolish mistake. I don't want to go into the details—if you are as much like me as I think you are, it would only tempt you to try the same experiment yourself.

Right now I just need to separate myself from the amulet for a little while.

I'm tired. Maybe with you tending the thing, I can finally rest.

I'll talk to you in the morning. In fact, with any luck, you will never have to read this letter. I will simply reclaim the amulet and dispose of it in some other way. (I did try to destroy it once. It was impossible!)

One other thing, in case you do read this: Don't let them get you down. You can be anything you want. Just believe in yourself.

Your loving aunt,
Zenobia

PS: Whatever you do, don't try to use the amulet!

6

DEATH DREAM

Other than the fact that she was totally unable to concentrate, returning to school was not as bad as Marilyn had feared. Her friends were sympathetic, and they spoke to her with a kindness that was often hidden in their day-to-day banter. Her teachers were willing to overlook her lack of attentiveness. And best of all, Kyle Patterson caught up with her on the way home, putting his baseball cap on her head and pulling the visor over her eyes.

"Wouldn't you rather be with Geoff?" she asked.

"I was thinking about your aunt. Geoff didn't understand Zenobia. You do." He blushed, and corrected himself. "Did."

Marilyn nodded. "I loved her." She heard her voice start to crack and turned away. She wasn't going to cry. Not now. Maybe not ever.

Kyle put an arm around her shoulder. "I know," he said. "I did, too."

She looked at him in surprise.

His blush deepened. "That may sound stupid. But I read all her books. I felt as if I knew her. And I wanted to be like her. I never admired anyone so much in my life."

Marilyn hesitated. For a moment she wondered if she should show him the letter, which had occupied center stage in her thoughts for the entire day.

She decided against it.

He'll just think Aunt Zenobia was losing her mind and end up feeling disillusioned. And that won't do anyone any good.

"What do you mean, you wanted to be like her?" she asked at last.

He tightened his mouth for a moment, and she was afraid he wasn't going to answer. Finally he said, "I don't usually talk about it, because I'm afraid people will laugh. But I'm thinking of becoming a writer. It's not the kind of thing you can just study and then go into, like carpentry or engineering. People seem to think you have to be weird to do it. But it's what I've always wanted. And knowing Zenobia ... well, she just made me feel like I could do it."

Marilyn was silent for a moment. She knew Kyle had just trusted her with a secret he wouldn't tell his best friends, not even Geoff.

"I know what you mean," she said at last. "At least, I think I do," she added quickly. She glanced up at him. He seemed to be waiting for her to go on. "I want to be a singer. Not just with a rock group. I want ... I want to be on Broadway."

There. It was out. A confidence for a confidence. He had trusted her, and she was responding in the only way she could think of—by trusting him, too.

But something inside her was waiting for him to laugh.

"I think you can do it," he said solemnly.

She looked at him in surprise.

"I've listened to you." He smiled at the blank look that crept into her features. "It was hard not to. You're always practicing in your room while Geoff and I are playing chess."

"You heard me?" she cried in horror. Blushing, but also smiling, she turned her head away. "I can't believe you could hear me."

"I *liked* hearing you," insisted Kyle. "I wouldn't just say that, because I know how hard it is to get the truth. But I like the way you sing. And I know a little about show music, because my old man is crazy for it and plays it all the time. So I think you can do it. And I want you to read a story I wrote," he continued breathlessly, "because maybe you'll tell me if you *don't* like it, which is something almost no one will do, and it would be great to have someone I could trust to tell me when something I do stinks. And . . ." And here he paused, taking a break in the flow of words that had been carrying him away.

She waited patiently.

"And I've been meaning to tell you," he said at last. "I really like you."

Marilyn's first surge of delight was replaced almost instantly by a flood of panic and the desperate thought, *What do I do now?*

Kyle reached for her hand. His own was warm and strong, and it made her feel safe.

She stopped worrying about what to do next. They walked home in a comfortable silence, feeling safe with each other's secrets. They lingered for a while on the front porch, then Kyle headed for home, and Marilyn slipped into the house.

Her sense of safety ended as soon as she entered and crossed the threshold.

Something was wrong.

She had no idea what it was ... or even why she was so sure of it, other than a prickling at the back of her scalp that made her want to turn and run.

She stood in the front hallway and listened. She could hear her mother singing to herself in the kitchen while she prepared dinner. It was a nice, homey sound that should have made her feel better.

It didn't.

The feeling persisted. Something was wrong.

Marilyn remembered a time when she was little and there had been a fire in the house's wiring. She had had the same vague sensation of fear then. As her parents had put it together later, she had smelled the smoke but hadn't known she was smelling it, because the odor was too weak to register at a conscious level. She had only known that something was wrong and had wandered around the house acting nervous and distracted for hours, complaining to her parents that she was frightened.

They had tried to calm her for a while, then finally they grew angry and told her to stop being foolish.

Ten minutes later the fire broke out in earnest.

She had the same kind of feeling now, an unmistakable sense that something was really wrong. She couldn't put her finger on what it was, because it was registering somewhere below the level of consciousness.

But it was there.

And she was frightened.

She went into the kitchen. Her mother was standing at the counter, peeling onions. "Grab a knife!" she said, tears streaming down her face. "It'll give you a good excuse to cry."

Mrs. Sparks believed that crying was good for the soul. Marilyn tended to think so, too, although she had not been able to cry over Zenobia—not since she had heard her voice. She was sure her mother was worried that she was "repressing her emotions," which had become one of her favorite phrases since she had heard a talk show about it a few months earlier.

Marilyn rummaged in a drawer by the sink and pulled out a paring knife. She picked up an onion.

"I don't know how your father does it," said her mother. "He's wonderful about sharing the work, but somehow he always manages to arrange the cooking schedule so that I do all the onions."

Marilyn smiled. But the vague feeling of uneasiness persisted.

When supper was in the oven, she headed for her room. As she reached the top of the stairs she could feel her apprehension increasing.

She was beginning to feel seriously frightened. What was causing this? Was it like the fire in the wiring? Was there something real, registering in her subconscious, warning her that something was wrong? Or was the feeling merely a reaction to everything that had happened in the last few days?

She stepped into her room. A little cry of fear broke from her lips and a thrill of horror shuddered down her spine. Every inch of her skin rose in goose bumps.

Someone had left her a message—scrawled it in dripping, blood-red letters on the mirror over her dresser:

GIVE IT BACK!

Marilyn lifted the back of her hand to her mouth and bit back a scream. For a moment she stood as if frozen.

Suddenly a welcome thought eased her tension. "It's a joke," she said out loud. "Stupid. But a joke."

She could see it now. Somehow Geoff had found out about the amulet and decided to give her a little scare. "He's the one Mom should be worrying about," she said to herself. "I don't know if he's 'repressing his emotions,' but I think he's getting a little too weird for normal people to deal with."

She walked toward the mirror, to see what Geoff had used to put the letters on with, wondering how much trouble it was going to be to clean them off.

She felt a little chill. Not only did they not smear when she ran her fingers over them, *she couldn't feel them at all!* The smooth surface of the glass was unmarked.

So how had Geoff put the message on? Suddenly Marilyn gave a cry of surprise and pulled her hand back as if she had been burned.

Watching in amazement, she saw the jagged, dripping letters fade from view. Within a few seconds the words were gone, the mirror as clear as if they had never been there.

All she saw when she looked into it now was her own face, staring back at her with eyes that were pools of fear.

A light rain pattered against the windshield of the car as the Sparks family drove to Flannigan's Funeral Parlor. Marilyn sat huddled in the backseat, still shaken by the incident with the mirror, uncertain whether the message had really been there or if she was simply losing her mind—and wondering which was more frightening.

They arrived in advance of the regular calling hours, and Mr. Flannigan ushered them into a long room. At one end of the room was Zenobia's coffin, surrounded by a startling number of floral arrangements. The bright profusion of gladiolus, roses, carnations, daisies, and lilies (not to mention at least a dozen varieties that Marilyn couldn't name) seemed an odd contrast to the solemn purpose of their visit.

Marilyn and her mother approached the coffin together. Marilyn was astonished when she saw Zenobia's body. Her aunt didn't look natural, or peaceful, or any of the other things her mother had told her people would say. She just looked infinitely better than she had the night she died. Marilyn wondered how the Flannigans had done that, then decided she didn't want to know.

She was surprised at how little she actually felt. Was it because she was numb, emotionally exhausted? Or was it because someplace deep inside of her she did not yet really believe that Zenobia was truly dead? That might explain the weird things that had happened in the last few days, including this afternoon's crazy experience with the mirror. Her mind was refusing to accept Zenobia's death; rather than deal with reality, it was playing tricks on her.

She felt an urge to reach out and touch her aunt in order to make the fact of her death more real, more understandable. She held back, more out of fear of what her mother might say than fear of actually touching the body.

Marilyn was so focused on trying to comprehend the fact of her aunt's death that it took her a moment to realize Zenobia was wearing the amulet. Several thoughts raced through her mind at once: How had it gotten here? Should she try to get it back? What would her mother say if she asked about it?

She settled them all with the thought that, given what Aunt Zenobia had said in her letter, perhaps the best thing to do with the amulet was bury it with her. At least then it would be in a place where it couldn't cause any more trouble.

She followed her mother back to the seats. Soon after, Mr. Flannigan opened the door and the visitors began to arrive, armed with condolences and curiosity.

Marilyn had already been introduced to a seemingly endless stream of cousins, aunts, uncles, and assorted shirttail relations when Kyle came in, looking very adult in his sport coat and tie. Marilyn was impressed; she had rarely seen him wear anything but T-shirts and jeans.

She watched him go to the coffin and stare morosely into it. When he came over to say hello to the family,

Marilyn caught a nod from her mother that temporarily excused her from the receiving line. Enormously grateful, she went to sit with Kyle.

Back at home, alone in her room, Marilyn slipped the cast recording of *Carousel* into her CD player. She flopped onto her bed and said, to no one in particular, "I never knew saying hello to long-lost relatives would be so tiring."

She kicked off her shoes and rolled onto her back. Brick jumped onto the bed and stared at her. Terrified that he was about to speak to her again, she moved to push him to the floor. She stopped herself, turning what was going to be a shove into a caress.

Don't punish the cat because you're *a nervous wreck,* she told herself severely.

As if to prove she had nothing to fear, Brick snuggled up next to her and began to purr.

On the disc the characters Julie Jordan and Billy Bigelow were singing her favorite romantic ballad: "If I Loved You." It was about two people trying hard to pretend not to be in love, and it always made her think of how she acted around Kyle.

She wondered if he ever felt that way, too.

She sighed.

The rest of the house was quiet.

Finally she began to drift toward sleep.

The dream began simply enough: She was in her bedroom. But she was outside herself, in the way you can be in dreams, watching herself sleep.

The dream-Marilyn tossed and turned fitfully, as if something were bothering her. Her hair was plastered to her forehead by an unhealthy sweat. She muttered constantly, words and thoughts that had no connection to one another.

Suddenly she knew, without knowing *how* she knew, that she was seeing the night of Zenobia's death.

What she saw next made her want to wake up.

Only when she tried, she found she couldn't. She was trapped in the dream, which was rapidly turning into a nightmare, and there was no way to get out of it.

"No," she murmured. *"No!"*

Her protest did no good. The dream continued. A helpless observer, she saw her dream-self roll onto its side, kicking at the covers. Then, her stomach knotting in fear, she watched one corner of her pillow lift itself up, moving as if pulled by an invisible hand.

Zenobia's amulet came sliding out from under the pillow.

The dream-Marilyn thrashed about on her bed, her sleep growing more restless.

The amulet floated across the room. Then the door opened, and the amulet was gone.

The scene of the dream changed abruptly, and she found herself in Zenobia's room.

Not merely in Zenobia's room. She was *in* Zenobia, seeing through Zenobia's eyes.

Her heart—Zenobia's heart—was pounding with terror.

It was the same night. The night of Zenobia's death.

Zenobia, and Marilyn with her, sat in bed, waiting. Somehow she knew something dreadful was approaching.

Before long, it arrived.

As Marilyn/Zenobia watched, body rigid, hands clamped like vises against her thighs, the door swung slowly open. And now, looking through Zenobia's eyes, Marilyn saw what she could not have seen with her eyes alone.

She saw the creature that had taken the amulet.

Skin crawling, she recoiled in horror from the monstrosity that approached the bed. It walked with a shuffling crouch, now like an ape, now like a man. Oddly, the claws of its feet made no sound on the hardwood floor.

The amulet dangled from its scaly fingers.

"Take it!" rasped the creature.

He extended a scaly, four-clawed hand. The amulet, catching a fragment of light from a nearby streetlamp, glittered in the darkness of the room.

"Take it!" he repeated. "You tried to thwart me, to hide it. It won't work. Take the amulet—so you can give it to *me!*"

Zenobia's hand reached forward and snatched the amulet from the creature.

"Now give it back!"

Marilyn would never have believed her aunt could be so frightened. But then, she would never have believed the world contained anything this frightful.

Zenobia's body trembled like a leaf in the wind. The creature leaned over her, its eyes blazing.

"Give me the amulet. *Give it to me!*"

In her dream Marilyn could feel Zenobia's heart— or was it her own?—pounding like a long-distance runner's.

The creature leaned closer. Its eyes were yellow and red, flickering like the fires of hell. Scaly skin, a dark red tinged with black, covered a body rippling with powerful muscles. Where its nose should have been were two pointed slits, a fringe of membrane rustling at their edges. Its snout jutted forward, curved fangs thrusting up from the lower jaw.

Leaning over the bed, the creature placed a powerful arm on either side of Zenobia's frail body, then said once more, "Give . . . me . . . the . . . amulet!"

And if Marilyn had been amazed at how frightened her aunt had been, she was even more astonished now at her bravery. With terror coursing through her veins, with a living nightmare leaning over her demanding the amulet, she tightened her grip on the golden chain and said, simply but firmly: "No."

Fire leaped in the creature's eyes. A look of rage contorted its hideous face.

"The amulet!" it roared. Its slash of a mouth drew open, and it lowered its face as though it were about to bite into Zenobia's neck.

Marilyn wanted to die.

Zenobia *did* die. The terror was finally too much, and her heart simply stopped beating.

7

GRAVE
CONVERSATIONS

With a cry of horror Marilyn wrenched herself out of the dream. She sat up in bed, her heart pounding. If that raging monster—jaws open, ready to bite—was the last thing Zenobia ever saw, then it was no wonder her face had been so twisted with fear.

"Now you know what happened that night," said a soft, familiar voice.

Marilyn gasped as Zenobia shimmered into sight at the foot of her bed.

"Please!" said Zenobia, her voice desperate. "Please, Marilyn, don't be frightened. I need your help. You have to get that amulet out of my coffin!"

This bizarre request did nothing to ease Marilyn's fear. But the need in Zenobia's voice was so real that she felt compelled to at least respond. Before she could think of what to say, Mrs. Sparks came running into the room. Her bathrobe dangled from one shoulder, and she fumbled with the other arm, trying to pull it on.

"Marilyn!" she cried. "Marilyn, what is it?"

Zenobia faded from view.

Marilyn shook her head. "I had a nightmare," she whispered, pressing her face into her hands.

Her mother sat on the bed next to her. "I'm sorry, honey," she whispered, slipping an arm around her shoulders.

They sat for a long time, neither of them speaking. Her mother held her close and rocked her gently.

"Of course, given all you've been through in the last few days, it's not surprising," said Mrs. Sparks at last. "To tell you the truth, I don't think I could have handled it as well as you did. That's part of what's helped me get through this, you know—thinking how brave you were that night when you found Aunt Zenobia. I keep telling myself that if you can hold up, I can, too."

Marilyn, leaning against her mother, turned and looked at her in surprise. That her mother was old-fashioned, even prudish, she had accepted long ago. That she would be bothered by Zenobia's death was a surprise to her.

"I thought you didn't like Aunt Zenobia."

Her mother seemed genuinely startled. "Whatever gave you that idea?" Before Marilyn could answer, Mrs. Sparks made a sad little noise in her throat. "Never mind. I *know* what gave you that idea. I didn't *act* much like I cared for her, did I?"

Marilyn shook her head. But she didn't say anything. She just wanted to feel her mother's presence right now, the way she had when she was little and something had frightened her. She was still trembling from the dream—and from what had happened after she woke up. For now it felt good to press against her mother. It helped her mind block out what she had seen. At the moment, that was the only way she could think of to deal with it: pretend it hadn't happened.

Part of her hoped if she pretended hard enough she could forget all about it.

Another part of her knew that was impossible.

"I *did* like her, you know," continued Mrs. Sparks, her voice defensive. "It's just that she was so ... I don't know. So *different*. Rowdy, almost. As if being a woman wasn't enough for her."

The defensive note had dropped away. Now her voice held only a trace of wistfulness. "I do know how you feel, Marilyn," she whispered. "Oh, yes, I do. Because when I was your age, there was nothing in the world I wanted more than to be like Aunt Zenobia."

Marilyn looked at her mother in astonishment.

"Don't be so surprised!" The tone in her voice was almost angry. "I'm human. I had dreams, too. But I grew up. That was something Zenobia never managed."

Any other time Marilyn would have argued with her mother. She didn't believe that growing up had to mean giving up. If becoming an adult meant letting go of your dreams, what good was it?

But right now she didn't want to argue. She just wanted to be held.

After a little while her mother began to hum

"Toora Lura Lura," a little lullaby she used to sing to Marilyn when she was very small. Marilyn hadn't heard it in years. She felt herself begin to relax.

After a while, she slept.

Mrs. Sparks continued to sit beside her for a long time, humming softly, tears rolling down her cheeks. Finally she sighed, wiped her eyes, and left the room.

When she was gone, Zenobia reappeared in the corner, and sat watching Marilyn sleep.

Friday was just like Thursday, a day to be passed through, endured.

Marilyn was vaguely aware of teachers talking. She knew she should be paying attention: final exams were coming up soon, and her grades were only so-so as it was. But somehow she couldn't bring anything into focus—any more than she could really relate to the friends who spoke to her, gently, kindly, throughout the day. All she could think of was Zenobia, and the amulet, and the horrible creature that had stalked through her dreams last night.

She was having a hard time sorting through everything. The dream about Zenobia she could understand. It made sense for her to be dreaming about her aunt right now. But where had that ... that *thing* come from?

It was worse—far worse—than any nightmare her mind had ever conjured up before. Even so, it was easy in the reassuring light of day to dismiss the creature as an invention of her overheated imagination.

What was not so easy was Zenobia. Not only was there the matter of her appearance *after* Marilyn had woken last night—an appearance Marilyn could not convince herself was just part of her nightmare, no matter how hard she tried—there was the fact that she had sensed Zenobia near her all through the day.

It was insane. But she couldn't shake the idea that her aunt was trying desperately to contact her.

"What do you want from me?" she wanted to scream.

But in her heart she already knew.

Zenobia wanted her to get the amulet.

But why? It must have something to do with the creature.

Again, her mind rebelled. Stretched to the limit, she was willing to admit the possibility of a ghost. The idea that someone who had "passed over" (to use a phrase she had heard almost endlessly during the last three days) could actually require something of someone still living was within her comprehension.

But that other thing? That creature? No. That had to be a figment of her imagination.

"You know, of course, my dear Airhead, that you've gone out of your miniature mind," said Alicia as they were walking home together.

Marilyn's heart sank. She had thought her old friend would be the one person she could confide in without ridicule.

"Oh, not because you think you've seen a ghost," said Alicia quickly. "I just meant you're out of your mind if you're starting to get serious about that dork Kyle Patterson. This problem with your aunt Zenobia, on the other hand, requires some serious consideration."

Marilyn smiled. She should have known Alicia wouldn't let her down.

"Now let me get this straight," continued her friend. "You think Zenobia's spirit is still hanging around."

"I've seen it."

Alice shrugged. "You see something worthwhile in that blond beanpole, too. Your eyesight is not the best."

"Lay off, will you?"

"Well, my credulity only goes so far. You can ask me to believe in a ghost, or you can ask me to believe that Kyle Patterson has redeeming features. I can't do both at once."

"Then I'll believe in Kyle all by myself," said Marilyn. "It's Aunt Zenobia who has me going in circles."

"Ah," said Alicia. "We return to the nub of the question. What do you suppose it is the old girl wants?"

"Her amulet," said Marilyn. "The one she asked me to take care of."

"Well, that makes sense. She asked you to take care of it, and now she wants it back. Why don't you just give it to her?"

"Because she already has it."

"I beg your pardon?"

"It's on her body, in the funeral home."

Alicia looked at her strangely. "Marilyn, what is this all about? What's the whole story?"

Marilyn looked away.

"Hey, Airhead—what is it?"

"You'll think I'm crazy."

Alicia snorted. "I *know* you're crazy. I figured that out sometime in third grade. That doesn't have anything to do with the current problem. Why does Zenobia want the amulet if she already has it?" She paused, then asked cautiously, "Is there more to this than just a ghost?"

Marilyn didn't answer for a long time. After they had walked three blocks in silence, she said, "Promise you won't laugh?"

Her face solemn, Alicia drew a cross over her heart, then placed her fingertip against her lips. It was a ritual they had developed years ago to ensure judgment-free listening.

Marilyn searched her friend's face. Alicia stared back at her with clear blue eyes.

"All right," said Marilyn at last. "I'll tell you everything that's happened. And if you ever tell anyone else, I'll kill you."

Alicia pointed to her mouth and moved her jaw as if she were trying to speak. Her lips remained sealed shut.

Marilyn smiled. But she remained silent for another moment. Overhead a cloud moved across the sun, blocking out the light. Marilyn shivered and began to speak, this time telling Alicia not merely that she had seen Zenobia's ghost, but all the details of the story, starting with the night that Zenobia had asked her to care for the amulet.

She went on to tell the story of the nightmare that had woken her the night of Zenobia's death—and of her horror at discovering the amulet she had been entrusted with was missing from her room. As she spoke, she realized for the first time that the creature she had seen in that first dream was the same one she had seen with the amulet last night. The knowledge had been there all along. She had been avoiding it, because she didn't want to deal with it.

She continued, telling Alicia about finding Zenobia's body, her hand still clutching the mysterious amulet, and the two voices she had heard at Zenobia's bedside.

Finally she told her about Zenobia's visit the night before.

Then she handed her Zenobia's letter.

Alicia read it, making little noises of astonishment as she went along. When she was done, she looked at Marilyn and said two things.

The first was: "I believe you."

The second was: "Boy, are you in trouble."

She was going to say more, but the cloud that had covered the sun was joined by several others. The sky opened and a slashing rain began to pour down on them.

Forgetting about the ghost, they ran for shelter.

They were in Alicia's bedroom, wearing bathrobes and toweling off their hair. Their clothes were down cellar in the dryer.

"The funeral is tomorrow," said Alicia. "That doesn't give you much time. Before you know it, Zenobia and the amulet will both be six feet under, and that'll be the end of the problem. Of course, her ghost might still hang around and kind of bug you. But she'll really have to stop harping on the amulet. I mean, gone is gone, and—"

"Alicia!"

"Sorry. I thought a little humor might be appreciated about now."

"It probably would have been," said Marilyn. "If you had managed to come up with any."

"So shoot me! I tend to talk when I get nervous."

"Also when you're calm. Besides, it's four, not six."

"Four what?"

"Four feet. That's how deep they dig graves around here. Five at the most. And they have this big concrete thing called a vault they put the coffin in to keep the wood from rotting."

"You amaze me. Whence comes this great knowledge of the funeral business?"

"My aunt just died, remember?"

"My uncle died last year, but I'm not ready to open a funeral parlor."

"Well, I've been paying close attention to the conversations my parents had with Mr. Flannigan. And I asked a few questions."

"Morbid curiosity," said Alicia. "A bad sign. All right, since you're such an expert, can you tell me why anyone should care if the wood rots once the coffin is planted?"

"I think it's in case they ever have to move the body—like if the state decided to put a highway through the cemetery or something. Maybe it's just to protect the family's investment in fine furniture. Anyway, by the time you get the top on the vault, there's less than three feet of dirt covering the thing. So it wouldn't be that hard to dig one up. Getting the top off the vault would be a problem, but—"

"Marilyn!"

"What?"

"Start over. Scratch that very bad, exceedingly stupid idea out of your mind. You sound like a clip from

Monster Movie Matinee. And I have no intention of playing Igor to some scatterbrained gravedigger on a midnight mission to the cemetery."

"Some henchperson you make. You'd better study your dwarf manual again."

"Look, Airhead, you start with the short jokes and you can face the unknown alone. Which is maybe not a bad idea. I don't know why I'm having this conversation with you at all."

"Because you're incredibly loyal. Anyway, I was just thinking out loud. Give me credit for a little common sense."

"I always did, until you started getting dopey about Kyle. A person who could take him seriously might do anything!"

"You want another short joke?"

"All right, all right! I'll lay off about Kyle. But what are you gonna do?"

"Do you suppose I could get the amulet off Zenobia's body during viewing hours tonight?"

"Possible, but not likely. How about if you just tell your mother you want it?"

"I tried. It was embarrassing. Not only did she think I was greedy, she thought I was 'excessively morbid.' "

"You could try telling her about the ghost."

Marilyn looked at Alicia.

"Yeah, I see what you mean," said Alicia. "Your mother already thinks your imagination is out of control. Hit her with this story and she's likely to decide the strain has been too much and you're ready for the funny farm. I mean, I only believe you because I have to."

"Thanks. I think."

"Anyway, to continue digressing, how did the amulet get on Zenobia to begin with?"

"Mr. Flannigan called Mom and asked her for something to 'finish the look.' She thought Zenobia was fond of the amulet, since she was clutching it when she died, and decided it would be a nice thing to have it buried with her. Sort of Egyptian, according to Mom."

Alicia raised an eyebrow. "That was nice of your mom, in a weird kind of way. But the whole thing still doesn't make sense. If your aunt was so fond of the amulet, why does she want you to get it off her?"

"Who knows why dead people do stuff?" said Marilyn, starting to feel exasperated.

Alicia shuddered, then whispered, "I've been pretty jokey about this. But the truth is, that's because you've got me scared. What do you think this is really all about?"

"I don't know."

"What are you gonna do?"

"I don't know," repeated Marilyn. "Nothing, if I'm lucky."

Alicia sighed. "Well, you know what to do if you need me."

Marilyn nodded. "I may take you up on that."

Alicia shuddered and sank back into her chair.

Outside, the rain fell in a slow, steady drizzle.

8

THE HAUNTED GHOST

Kyle showed up at the funeral parlor again that night, as did a number of writers and editors who had worked with Zenobia at one time or another. They had flown in that day in order to be present at the funeral Saturday morning.

Surrounded by what seemed like mountains of flowers, their odor almost overwhelming her, Marilyn stood at Zenobia's coffin and looked down at her aunt. The amulet rested on her chest, partially covered by a small bouquet of roses and baby's breath. As she looked at it now, the smooth, blue edge peeking out from under a curling petal, she had an almost irresistible urge to reach down and snatch it.

She glanced around. No one was watching.

She shook herself. Craziness! All it would take

would be one person turning in her direction, and there would be an uproar, followed by embarrassment and humiliation, and the rest of her natural life in therapy.

She looked down at Zenobia again. Her sharp features were waxy with the pall of death. *Why are you doing this to me?* thought Marilyn fiercely. *What is this all about?*

To her horror, Zenobia answered her. The words came as a whisper in the back of her mind: *Be patient, Marilyn. Be patient, and brave. I need you.*

The combination of staring at her aunt's dead body and hearing her voice at the same time was too much for Marilyn. She gripped the edge of the coffin as her knees started to buckle. For a horrible instant the coffin wobbled. Marilyn gasped. She thought it was going to tip over, and her mind conjured up a gruesome picture of Zenobia's body falling out and pinning her to the floor.

Her mind continuing to run wild, she wondered if she could snatch the amulet if that happened.

All at once Kyle was at her side. Slipping his arm around her shoulders, he led her back to her chair, supporting her as he did. A small circle of concerned people quickly formed around them.

Suddenly she saw her father come pushing through the crowd, shouldering aside assorted cousins. To her enormous relief he shooed the entire group away, bellowing, "Give her some room to breathe, for Pete's sake!"

He used the fierce voice he generally reserved for his high school students, which caused the murmuring relatives to pull back in astonishment. Standing at a respectful distance, they watched her from the corners of their eyes.

"Hot night," said her father gruffly. "Too much going on. You okay, Marilyn?"

She nodded weakly.

"Good." He took out his handkerchief and wiped his brow. "Take her outside for a while, would you, Kyle?"

"Yes sir," said Kyle. Putting his hand on Marilyn's elbow, he led her through the crowd to the front porch. The air was indeed warm, and still muggy from the afternoon rain. But a gentle breeze offered some relief, and as it lifted the damp strands of coppery hair from her shoulders, Marilyn realized for the first time how stuffy the big room had actually been.

Kyle let go of her elbow. Then he took her hand and led her to the large oak tree at the corner of Flannigan's lawn.

"Okay," he said. "Spill."

"Spill?" asked Marilyn nervously, though she knew perfectly well what he meant.

"Something is really messing you up. And it's not just your aunt's death, though Lord knows that would be enough. But I've been watching you. You are seriously spooked. I've known you too long not to see it. So just spill it, will you? We'll both feel better."

Oh, Kyle, she thought desperately. *How I wish I could. But I don't dare. It's too crazy. You could never believe me.*

Out loud she said, "You're wrong. It *is* Aunt Zenobia. It was all so sudden, and I really miss her, and being the one to find her was just so weird."

Which is pretty much the truth, she told herself, try-

73

ing to salve the way her conscience was complaining about the lie.

Kyle looked at her suspiciously. "That's all?"

She nodded. "You know how I felt about her. The loss is hard to take."

His eyes, fringed with golden lashes and bluer than a summer sky, peered into hers, searching for something.

"Will you call me if I can help you?" he asked at last.

"Yes," she said simply. "If I think you can help, I'll call."

But I don't think you can. I don't think anyone can help me now. Because either I'm being haunted or I'm losing my mind. And those are both things you do alone.

Of course, she wasn't really alone, Marilyn thought later, sitting in her room. She had Alicia. But she wasn't sure how much of this Alicia believed. She had a feeling her friend was merely humoring her.

She looked around her room. It was familiar, comfortable. She had slept in it all her life.

But she no longer felt safe here, which was why she was awake now, even though she needed sleep so desperately that her eyes were stinging. She was too afraid to sleep. When she stretched out on her bed, her body was as rigid as a board. Her eyes, as if they were out of her control, refused to close. The book she had been trying to read lay on the floor beside her chair. She had been totally unable to concentrate on it.

Brick jumped up and sat in her lap. She reached

down and stroked his head. But she could feel the tension that had formed in her shoulders at his approach. She was still afraid of the cat, and that made her sad. Brick began to purr, pushing his head insistently against her hand to demand more attention.

The clock in the downstairs hall chimed three.

A moment later Zenobia walked through the door.

Brick yowled in protest as Marilyn's hands clutched his body. She felt a cold sweat pop out on her brow. She wasn't dreaming, or just waking up, or just drifting off. All the reasons she might use to explain things away were worthless here. She was wide awake, and the woman who was lying in a coffin at Flannigan's Funeral Home had just walked through her door—which was still closed, now that she glanced at it.

She tried to say something, but her throat seemed sealed shut, her mouth as dry as a day old doughnut.

Zenobia spoke instead. "Don't be afraid."

Though it was clearly her voice, the words didn't seem to come from Zenobia's lips. Instead, they whispered inside Marilyn's head.

Marilyn remained rigid, fear winning out over desire. For part of her wanted to rush to her aunt and fling her arms around her. Another part, stronger, wanted this awful thing to disappear forever and leave her alone.

"It's difficult," said the voice in her mind. "I know you don't understand. But I need your help."

Marilyn nodded.

"You know what you have to do?" asked Zenobia.

She nodded again, then said, "What I don't understand is *why*."

Zenobia sighed. "Because if I am buried with that

75

amulet, I will never be allowed to rest. Guptas will see to that. He'll haunt me and harass me through all eternity."

"Who is Guptas?"

"The prisoner of the amulet. Listen quickly. I would come with you, if I could. But this appearing act takes a lot out of me, and I can't keep it up very long. I'm hoping I'll get better at it as times goes on."

Zenobia was already beginning to fade. But Marilyn had one last question, the most important one of all as far as she was concerned. "Are you real?" she whispered desperately.

Dumb! she thought as soon as she had asked it. *Do you expect a hallucination to tell you it's imaginary?*

"As real as tomorrow," replied the voice in her mind.

Marilyn relaxed a little. That was the kind of thing Zenobia would say. And not the kind of thing she, Marilyn, would think of on her own.

So maybe this really was Zenobia's ghost.

With a start Marilyn realized she was glad the ghost was real. She had been half convinced she was losing her mind . . . a prospect she found far more frightening than a mere ghost.

"I have to go now," said Zenobia. "I'll come back as soon as I can." Her figure wavering in the air, growing mistier by the second, she took a step toward Marilyn. Holding her hands out beseechingly, she added, "Don't let me down."

Then she was gone.

But one last thought hung in Marilyn's mind, one last message from Zenobia's spirit. The words had formed even as her image disappeared. And, it seemed to Marilyn, they left her no choice.

"I'm counting on you," she had said.

Marilyn looked around at the empty room. Brick was still on her lap, but he had risen to his feet, and his back was arched like a cat in a Halloween picture. Suddenly she realized he had sunk his claws into her leg. She cried out in pain and swatted at him. He turned and hissed at her, then jumped off her lap and ran under the bed.

She rubbed her leg, wondering how she had ignored the pain until now.

Forget it, she ordered herself. *You've got work to do.*

She slipped into her jeans and a sweatshirt, dug her sneakers from under the bed, then went to her nightstand and took out her flashlight.

This was going to be dark work. She hoped she wouldn't have an attack of her nightfrights.

Glancing nervously around her room, she tried to convince herself to give up the whole crazy idea. But she had promised her aunt. And if she wanted to grow up to be the kind of person Zenobia had been, she couldn't wimp out now.

With a sigh, she stepped through the door.

Save for the distant rumble of her father's snoring, the house was quiet. She turned on her flashlight and walked carefully down the hallway, moving as silently as possible.

A few moments later she stood on the front porch. She felt a twinge of sorrow as she remembered Zenobia standing there, smoking her cigar and telling outrageous stories.

She started down the steps and almost tripped over Brick, who had slipped out the door with her.

"Watch out, stupid," she hissed as the cat wound himself between her feet. He bared his little teeth at her and bounded down the steps.

The night was cooler now, and very still, except for the breeze, which continued to blow gently through the town, carrying the fragrance of a dozen different kinds of flowers that had come into bloom that week.

The sky was clear, moonless but filled with glittering stars.

It was almost too perfect and Marilyn felt a sudden surge of affection for this little corner of the world that she had so often found unbearably boring. After the last few days she was beginning to think that boring wasn't such a bad thing.

Looking around now at the simple, familiar surroundings, it was hard to believe she was on her way to a funeral home to steal an amulet from the chest of a corpse.

Panic gripped her. She wanted to turn back.

"I'm counting on you," echoed a voice in her memory.

She squared her shoulders and started down the walk.

When she reached the corner, a figure glided from the shadows beneath one of the street's old oak trees.

Making no sound, it followed her into the night.

9

MIDNIGHT MOVES

Flannigan's Funeral Home was some fifteen blocks from Marilyn's house. Streetlamps stood at most of the corners, but there were patches of darkness in between. Marilyn focused on the pools of light and set them as goals while she walked through the dark areas. Her old fear of the dark kept trying to rise within, and her heart fluttered against her breastbone like a trapped bird.

Just as she was beginning to think the trip would take forever, she reached the last block before Flannigan's—at which point she realized she was actually going to arrive much too quickly for her taste. She suddenly wished the funeral home were still miles away.

She glanced around and noticed a car traveling

slowly in her direction. As she had twice before during the trip, Marilyn stepped back from the sidewalk. The people who roamed the streets at night frightened her.

Hypocrite, she thought. *You're out roaming the streets, too.* She smiled in spite of herself. *Geez, given what I'm up to, whoever's in that car is probably more normal than I am!*

She began to catalog the possibilities: a tired mother on her way home from her second shift job; some crazed party animal who lived by night; or (getting romantic) some heartbroken lover whose tragedy denied him (or her!) the solace of sleep.

How weird is that, compared to someone who's out to rob a corpse? she demanded of herself.

After the car passed her, she counted to twenty. Moving carefully, checking to be sure it really was gone, she stepped back onto the sidewalk.

When she reached the funeral home a moment later Marilyn tucked her flashlight into the back pocket of her jeans. Terrified or not, this had to be done in darkness. That also meant she didn't dare risk trying the front door, since a bright light burned in the porch ceiling.

Moving quietly, she went around to the back of the building, hoping she wouldn't have to break a window, or anything stupid like that.

She also hoped there was no one here. She knew Mr. Flannigan sometimes worked late. That would be all she needed—to run into the undertaker while she was trying to rob one of his corpses!

At least the Flannigans didn't actually *live* here anymore. The youngest Flannigan boy, Richie, was in her class, and she still remembered coming to his eighth birthday party, back when the family had been living on the upper floor of the big old house. For years afterward she had wondered what it was like to live in a place like this.

She had wanted to ask Richie, but had been too shy to do it, partly because he was such a nice, normal kid and she didn't want to embarrass him. But looking at the house now, the questions came back to her again.

Do the spirits of the newly dead wait here until they're buried? How many ghosts would a funeral parlor attract, anyway?

She shivered and pushed the thoughts from her mind.

The backyard was dark. Too dark. A wave of panic seized her, and she stood for a moment as if frozen. She reached for the flashlight, thinking, *If I get caught, I get caught. I can't go any farther without some light!*

The grass, which had not been mowed back here, was wet with dew. She could feel it beginning to soak through her sneakers. Moving the beam of the flashlight, she picked out the back porch.

Cautiously she climbed the steps.

The door was locked. She rattled the handle hopelessly, then stopped because she realized it was making a loud noise.

She turned and caught her breath. She could have sworn she saw a movement in the row of lilacs separating Flannigan's lawn from the next house.

Holding her breath, she swept her flashlight back and forth across the bushes. When she couldn't see a thing, she cursed the flashlight for being too weak and tried to convince herself it was just nerves.

Don't be foolish, she chided herself. *No one else would be dumb enough to be out here at this time of night anyway!*

But the seed had been planted. She couldn't shake the suspicion that something was watching her.

Her nervousness doubled, she turned back to the house.

How on earth do I get in?

Playing the beam along the wall, she noticed a row of windows leading into the basement.

Maybe one of them would be unlatched.

She went to the corner of the house and started working her way along the wall.

She couldn't believe her luck. Not only was the third window unlatched—it was broken right out. The hole was covered by a sheet of thick plastic, the kind people put over their windows in winter to try to keep the heat in. It was held on by strips of thin wood tacked to the frame with small nails.

She put her fingers at the edge and tried to pull the wood away.

It wouldn't budge.

She put her fingernails against the plastic and tried to rip through it.

Nothing. Made to stand up against fierce winter winds, the stuff was impervious to her efforts. For the first time, she envied those girls who took pride in long pointed nails.

"Here," said a voice behind her. "Try this knife."

Marilyn screamed. The flashlight flew out of her hand and bounced off the wall. She spun about and put her back to the house, as if it could somehow protect her.

"You!"

Kyle Patterson smiled. "None other. What in blazes are you up to?"

"Go away," said Marilyn.

The smile faded from Kyle's face. "Not a chance. You're in some kind of trouble—or you're going to be, if you get caught. I'm not leaving you alone here. So you may as well let me help."

"You can't. And I can't explain. You'll think I'm crazy."

"Marilyn!" He took a deep breath and lowered his voice. "I *know* you're crazy. That's not the point. I'm on your side. Whatever it is you've gotten yourself mixed up in, I want to help." He looked at her, and his eyes were almost fierce. "I mean it!"

She leaned against the wall and let out her breath with a heavy sigh. "You don't know what you're saying."

"I don't care what it is!" Dropping the knife he had offered her, he reached forward and took her by the shoulders. For a moment she thought he was going to shake her. "I don't care what it is," he repeated, drawing her closer.

She collapsed against his chest and, to her own astonishment, began to cry.

He put his arms around her and held her close. "You don't even have to tell me," he whispered, his voice gentle. "Just let me help."

She nodded and pressed against him.

"All right, I will. You don't know how scared I've been, Kyle. You don't know how awful these last days have been. I should make you go, now, before it's too late ... before you're tangled up in this, too. But I can't. I'm too scared."

He tightened his arms around her. "It'll be all right," he whispered. "Whatever it is, it'll be all right."

She drew back from him and wiped her eyes. "What are you doing here, anyway?"

"I couldn't sleep."

She looked at him suspiciously.

He sighed. "All right, if you want the truth, I talked to Alicia. She told me you might be doing something crazy."

Marilyn scowled.

"Don't be angry with her. It just about killed her to call me. But she didn't know what else to do. And even then she wouldn't tell me what this is all about. She just told me you might need help." He took a deep breath. "Which is why I'm here."

She stared at him for a long time.

"All right," she said at last. "If you mean it, let's get busy. We don't have much time."

"What are we going to do?"

She took a deep breath, then said, "I'm here to rob a corpse."

Before he could reply, she bent and picked up the pocketknife he had dropped. Turning back to the window, she opened the long, sharp blade, hesitated, then closed it again. Using the short blade, which was blunt, she was able to pry the wood framing loose from the sill without tearing the plastic.

"Here, let me finish that," said Kyle. Reaching past her, he tucked his fingertips over the top of the wood and pulled. His arm was close to her face and she couldn't help noticing the play of his muscles and the faint scent of sweat on his skin.

"There!"

The strip of wood ripped away from the wall, bringing the plastic with it. He made a few more quick tugs, and the window was clear.

Marilyn looked at the opening and shuddered. It was like a black mouth leading into emptiness.

Kyle put his hand on her shoulder. "I'll go first."

She shook her head. "This is my problem. I go first."

"Suit yourself." She could sense the shrug of his shoulders.

She looked at the hole again and wished he had been willing to fight her for the point. *Too late now, Sparks. Get moving!*

She picked up her flashlight from where it had fallen in the wet grass and played the beam through the window. The light revealed a small room walled in by planks of aged wood. The walls were covered with shelves, the shelves filled with bottles of different kinds—the tools of Mr. Flannigan's trade.

"Here goes nothing," she whispered, slipping her feet through the window.

A moment later she was inside, and a moment after that Kyle was standing beside her, his arm around her shoulders again. "Now what?" he whispered.

"We go upstairs," she answered. "Where they keep the bodies."

10

ROBBING THE DEAD

It was a gruesome passage. Mr. Flannigan had his working space here in the cellar, and they had to pass through it as they made their way to the first floor.

Marilyn clung tightly to Kyle's arm as he swung the beam of her flashlight back and forth, trying to find the stairway. Two tables with white sheets spread over them had distinctive outlines that made her shudder. She tried to think of who had died lately, then tried to push the question out of her mind. She didn't want to know who was lying cold, naked, and dead beneath those sheets.

The whole place had the air of death about it. She found herself afraid to touch things, plagued by the feeling that the essence of death would rub off on her, and that she might never be able to wash it away.

Suddenly Kyle stopped. "What was that?" he hissed.

"What was what?" she replied, feeling a little like a second-rate comic in a horror-film spoof.

"I thought I heard something behind us."

They stood motionless, holding their breath while they waited for another sound.

They heard nothing.

"Probably just my nerves," said Kyle.

"You're nervous?" asked Marilyn, a little incredulously. It had never occurred to her that anything would frighten Kyle.

"I'm scared silly!" he snapped. "If I wasn't so worried about you, I wouldn't be anywhere near here!"

She pulled a little closer to him. "Thanks," she whispered.

"Don't mention it. Let's get this over—"

His words were cut off by a loud crash. Marilyn let out a shriek and clutched Kyle's arm as if it were a life preserver. He, in turn, threw his other arm around her and pulled her close to him. They stood for a moment in absolute silence, straining their ears for whatever had caused the noise.

Suddenly Marilyn began to giggle.

"What's so funny?" demanded Kyle.

"That," she said, pointing to their left.

Kyle swung the flashlight in the direction she indicated. The beam was reflected by a pair of greenish eyes.

"Brick!" he said in disgust. "The world's clumsiest cat."

"He must have followed me," said Marilyn. "I wonder what he broke. I hope it wasn't important." Gesturing to the cat, she called, "Come here, Brick. Come here, kitty."

Brick padded over and rubbed against her legs. She reached down and scooped him up. "You're coming with us," she said. "The last thing I need is to leave here tonight with you still inside for Mr. Flannigan to find in the morning."

Brick purred and snuggled up against her.

"Come on," she said to Kyle. "Let's get this over with before anyone else shows up. For a solo expedition, this has gotten pretty crowded."

"You want me to leave?"

"Don't you dare! Just find that stairway."

As it turned out, he had already located it while she was fooling with the cat. Taking her by the elbow again, he led her to a set of solid wooden steps.

"They're sturdier than you would think, considering the house," said Marilyn.

"Not when you consider what they're used for," replied Kyle grimly.

Marilyn glanced back at the tables and shuddered. They climbed the rest of the stairs in silence.

The first floor of Flannigan's was divided into three major areas. Each was currently in use.

"Which way from here?" asked Kyle, shining his beam along the faded carpet in the hallway.

"I don't know," said Marilyn. "I'm confused."

"You've spent the last two evenings here!"

"I know, but I never got back to this part!"

They went through a door on their left.

Kyle played the flashlight slowly over the room. A ring of floral arrangements surrounded a small white casket at the far end. "Billy Johnson," he said, his voice husky,

Marilyn turned away. Billy Johnson was a third

grader who lived a few blocks from her. He had been killed the previous afternoon in a car crash. "Let's get out of here," she said.

They went back into the hall. "That's it!" said Marilyn, spotting a familiar doorway.

Kyle pushed it open. Marilyn felt a tingle of anticipation.

The room, empty now, seemed strange to her. For two nights she had seen it alive with people; friends, relatives—even strangers who cared, for one reason or another, about Zenobia.

Now there was no one here but Zenobia herself.

Marilyn hesitated for a moment. Suddenly she had an awful fear that everything—all the crazy events of the last few days—had been nothing but a product of her overactive imagination, stimulated by her sorrow over Zenobia's death.

What am I doing here? she thought in panic. The answer that she was here because Zenobia had asked her to be suddenly seemed wildly inadequate. She was here to rob a corpse, and that was that.

"Are you all right?" asked Kyle.

"No."

"Can I help?"

"No."

He let his hand rest against the small of her back and was quiet.

Marilyn was weighing the alternatives. Part of her was terrified that she would go home with Zenobia's amulet in her hand and find that everything had been hallucinations after all. She might never get caught with it. Even if she did she could make the point that Zenobia had given her the amulet.

But whether or not she got in trouble wasn't the point. The point was, in her heart she would know what she had done. In her heart she would remember robbing the dead for as long as she lived.

In fact, she could think of only one thing worse: going home without the amulet and finding it had all been real, and she had let Zenobia down.

In the end there was no choice: She had to do it.

"Stay here," she whispered to Kyle. Taking the flashlight from his hand, she walked toward the coffin. The scent of the flowers was overwhelming, almost sickening in its sweetness.

She hesitated, remembering the moment earlier that evening when she had heard Zenobia's voice. Would it happen again?

She braced herself and stepped forward. Her light hit Zenobia's face, etching her still, cold features against the coffin's satin lining.

She took another step.

There it was! The beam of her light had caught the edge of the amulet.

Now there was nothing to it. All she had to do was reach down and take it.

She couldn't.

She remembered her aunt pleading with her earlier in the evening.

She couldn't let her down now.

Slowly she forced herself to reach out and move aside the spray of flowers that covered the amulet. The red jewel in the center caught her light and sprang to life, as if it were filled with a fire of its own.

When nothing else happened, she began to relax a

bit. She had almost expected a clap of thunder and a heavenly voice chastising her for robbing the dead.

She took a breath and reached down to lift the amulet from Zenobia's chest.

Something was wrong. It took her a moment to figure it out. Then she realized—Zenobia was dead, and being dead was cold. Yet the amulet was warm, warmer, even, than if it had been resting on the chest of a living person.

Marilyn shivered. What was this thing, anyway?

Then a worse question occurred to her. How was she going to get it off Zenobia's corpse? The chain, she now remembered, had no clasp. It was a solid piece of work.

You've come this far, Sparks, she told herself firmly. *No sense in being squeamish now.*

She set the flashlight in the coffin. The beam, playing around the amulet, cast eerie shadows on Zenobia's waxy-looking face, and the wall of flowers behind her.

Marilyn reached down and slipped her hand under the corpse's head. She tried to tip the neck forward.

It wouldn't bend.

She remembered what she had heard about rigor mortis and the stiffness of death. Pulling harder, she was able to raise Zenobia's entire body just enough to free the chain. She was amazed at how light, even frail, her tough old aunt seemed now.

Bracing her left elbow against the side of the coffin, Marilyn held Zenobia's body at a slight angle. Then she took the amulet in her right hand and guided the loop of the chain under the back of Zenobia's head. She moved slowly, trying not to disturb the carefully arranged white hair. Once the chain was free, she continued to slide it along her own arm, until it reached the crook of her elbow. Then she let it dangle against the outside of the casket while she put her hand back under Zenobia's head and gently lowered the body to a resting position.

She had done it!

She grabbed the flashlight and turned triumphantly to Kyle, holding up the amulet. "I've got it!" she whispered. "I've got . . ."

Her words faltered, trailed to a whisper. Kyle was staring at her in horror.

No. He wasn't staring at her. It was something behind her.

She heard a soft noise and whirled around.

Zenobia had placed one hand on each side of the coffin and was drawing herself to a sitting position.

Marilyn's throat closed with fear. She was trying desperately to scream, but nothing would come out.

Zenobia was sitting straight up now. Still moving stiffly, her torso twisted in their direction.

The corpse opened its eyes and looked at Marilyn. A hideous smile twisted its face. Reaching out with its cold, white hands, it said, "Give me the amulet."

Marilyn dropped the flashlight.

It clattered to the floor and went out. Except for a faint glow coming from the amulet itself, the room was pitch black.

But she could hear the sound of fabric rustling, and there was no question in her mind what it meant.

Zenobia was climbing out of her coffin.

11

THE EYE OF
THE AMULET

The darkness was driving Marilyn out of her mind. She couldn't see a thing. Not a thing!

But the sound of the slow, deliberate movements of whatever had climbed out of Zenobia's casket fueled her imagination, and she could almost see the dead eyes looking into hers, feel the cold hands closing on her neck.

Unable to think of anything else to do, she started to sing.

Later, she could never understand exactly why she reacted that way. At the moment she didn't even think about it. It just happened. She opened her mouth to scream, some instinct took over, and the words to "When You Walk Through a Storm"—the anthem of hope in the midst of darkness from *Carousel*—started pouring out instead.

The funny thing was, it worked. She actually felt better, at least for the first few notes.

Better yet, the noise in front of her stopped.

Unfortunately, the moment of relief was short-lived. She had just reached the line "And don't be afraid of the dark" when a harsh voice grated, "Silence, wench! Hand me that amulet!"

At that moment the terror she had been fighting to stave off all night finally came crashing in on her. Her old fear of the dark was multiplied a thousandfold by all the genuine horrors she had had to face, and she began to scream, hopelessly and uncontrollably. Somewhere in the background she could hear Kyle. She thought he was screaming, too, but she couldn't be certain.

"Silence!" ordered the voice again.

The scream died in Marilyn's throat. She was too frightened to force it out.

The amulet was burning in her hand.

Suddenly it blazed into life. A red glow burst from the jewel in its center. By its fiery light she could see Zenobia's corpse standing in front of the coffin.

"Give me the amulet!" repeated the voice. The corpse began lurching toward her, its pale white fingers twitching with anticipation.

"Marilyn, let's get out of here!"

It was Kyle. His wits had finally returned, and he was beside her, his hands on her shoulders, trying to turn her around.

It did no good. She was rooted to the spot, mesmerized by the horror moving step by step in her direction.

"Marilyn!"

"Give ... me ... the amulet!"

The corpse was almost upon them now. They could see, by the amulet's glow, a look of something close to madness in its eyes.

Kyle put his arm around Marilyn's waist and pulled her back. He tried to run, but got no help from her. He turned and linked both hands around her stomach, then began backing toward the door.

"There is no use in fleeing. There is nowhere to run! Give me the amulet!"

Suddenly Marilyn began to struggle with Kyle. "Let go of me!" she cried, twisting in his arms.

Zenobia's corpse, moving slowly, was almost upon them.

The glare from the amulet was brighter than ever.

Kyle tightened his grip; spurred by terror, he lurched backward. As he did, he stepped on Brick, who had been lurking behind him. The cat emitted a piercing yowl of pain and shot away to hide under one of the chairs. But the damage had been done; Kyle's footing had been destroyed. He struggled wildly to keep his balance, but finally failed and fell backward, still holding Marilyn.

Her feet thrust out and tangled in Zenobia's legs, causing the corpse to fall on top of them.

When her aunt's body landed on her, Marilyn screamed, convinced she was going to die of fright if nothing else.

The corpse reared back and opened its mouth. With a fresh jolt of horror Marilyn realized it was going to bite her. She thrust upward with her palm, catching Aunt Zenobia's body under the chin, slamming her head back. "Oh! I'm so sorry!" she gasped.

The corpse howled with rage and began to scrabble at her hand, trying to rip the amulet from her fingers. Marilyn beat at it with her fists, trying to push it away. She was still screaming and crying.

Kyle, pinned beneath both of them, struggled to free himself so he could help Marilyn.

The whole scene was illuminated by the bloody red light still pulsing from the amulet.

"Guptas, let go of that body!"

The voice was Zenobia's, but it did not come from her body. Looking in the direction from which it had come, Marilyn was astonished to see another version of her aunt standing next to them. She had her hands on hips. A furious expression contorted her face. And her body, rather than solid and heavy like the corpse with which Marilyn was now wrestling, was clearly that of a ghost.

"Guptas, let go!" repeated Zenobia.

A howl of despair ripped through the night. Suddenly Zenobia's corpse went limp, trapping Kyle and Marilyn under its dead weight. The light in the amulet died, so that the only illumination in the room came from the pale figure of Zenobia, who was still scowling.

"I hate to see that body treated that way," she said bitterly. "It served me very well for quite a number of years. And you be careful there, young man!" This last was addressed to Kyle, who was trying to roll the corpse away so that he and Marilyn could sit up.

Zenobia's ghost turned and walked toward the coffin, which had shifted when the corpse climbed out of it. Reaching out, she tried to move it back into place.

Nothing happened, and she made a little noise of frustration.

"Well, at least we have the amulet back," she said, turning her back to the coffin.

"Will you help us get out from under this?" asked Kyle, his voice testy.

"I can't!" snapped Zenobia. "I haven't learned how to move things yet. It's all I can do to materialize."

Marilyn, still in a daze, began to come to her senses. Gently she helped Kyle push Zenobia's now empty body away from them. Then she shoved the amulet into her pocket, got to her feet, and reached down to help him up.

When he was standing beside her, she turned to her aunt. "Don't you vanish on me this time," she said. Though she was trembling, her voice had an angry tone, and her jaw was set in a firm line that made it look remarkably like Zenobia's. "I think it's about time you filled me in on a few things!"

"You're right," said Zenobia, looking a little shamefaced. "I should have before. Only I didn't know much. I only had guesses. I still don't understand all of it, but I'm beginning to make sense of things."

She looked around nervously. "We'll have to hurry. We won't have much time before it starts again."

Kyle and Marilyn glanced at each other. "Before *what* starts again?" asked Marilyn.

"Sit down," said Zenobia. "I want to tell you a story."

Kyle went to the row of chairs that had been set up for calling hours. He picked up two, then turned back to Zenobia and asked, uncertainly, "Do you want one?"

Zenobia shrugged. "I have no need to take the weight off my feet," she said with the ghost of a smile. "I'll stand."

Kyle returned with chairs for himself and Marilyn. He placed them side by side, then took Marilyn's hand. The two of them sat down together.

"Damn!" said Zenobia. "This isn't going to be easy. I wish I had a cigar."

"We can do without the smell," said Marilyn impatiently. "Let's get on with this."

"Aren't we touchy?" said Zenobia.

"Considering that I'm sitting in a funeral parlor, which I broke into, in the middle of the night, and having a conversation with a ghost whose body just tried to kill me, I think I'm doing pretty well! Tell me you had an experience that topped this one in all your famous travels."

She was holding Kyle's hand with a crushing grip and pressing herself against him to keep the violence of her trembling from being too visible.

Zenobia shook her head. "Nope. You've got me on that one. I've been almost everywhere and never had an experience to top this one. Nothing like your own hometown for a good time."

Marilyn made a sound of exasperation.

"All right, all right," said Zenobia. "I'll get on with it. But this isn't easy, because a lot of it's my own fault, and I'm going to have to admit to screwing up in a way that I'm not used to."

She looked wistfully down to where her body lay on the floor. "If I'd handled things a little better, I might still be inside that, instead of struggling with all my might just to stay visible for you." She shrugged. "But that's neither here nor there. What you want to know is, what's going on."

Marilyn nodded.

"Well, I don't know," said Zenobia flatly. "At least, not entirely. But I can tell you this much: That amulet is haunted by a demon named Guptas, who was bound to it by the great Suleiman himself.

"What Guptas wants most of all is to be free. But he is subject to whoever owns the amulet. If you know how to use it, you can command incredible power.

"But that's the problem: knowing how to use it. If you try to summon Guptas without knowing the proper procedures, you can end up in big trouble."

"Which is what happened to you?" asked Marilyn.

Zenobia nodded sheepishly. "I really should have known better. Even though I'd never seen anything like that in action, I've spent enough time in the ancient parts of the world to know what can happen. There are strange stories—things *we* would call primitive nonsense—that crop up over and over, linger in the mind, have touches that just don't want to let you explain them away. I should have known better than to fool around with this thing after Eldred died."

"Eldred Cooley?" asked Kyle.

"Yes," said Zenobia with a scowl. "If I ever catch up with him, I swear . . ."

Marilyn caught her breath as a second form shimmered into sight beside Zenobia. "Don't!" it said sharply. "Don't swear to anything, Zenobia. You have no idea how binding an oath is for someone in our condition."

Marilyn had seen Zenobia angry before. She had seen her, in the last week, frightened. But she had never seen her quite this surprised.

"Eldred Cooley!"

The figure standing before them was a small, dapper-looking man. He was slightly overweight, slightly balding, and somewhere, Marilyn guessed, slightly over the age of fifty. Or at least, he had been when he died.

"What is going on here?" asked Kyle. Marilyn squeezed his hand. He sounded like a little kid who had lost his mother in a department store.

Nobody answered him. The two ghosts were looking at each other with an expression Marilyn could not decipher, though it seemed to contain elements of respect, anger, and longing in equal measure.

"Well, what are *you* doing here, Eldred?" asked Zenobia at last.

"The same thing you are," answered Cooley. "Trying to make up for past mistakes."

Marilyn felt Brick rubbing about her legs. She reached down to pick him up and suddenly felt the hair on the back of her neck begin to rise. She sat up straight, the cat still in her hands, and said, "Danger!"

Even as the word left her lips, a searing heat burst against her leg. The amulet had blazed into life again.

Eldred Cooley shouted something in a language that sounded unlike any she had ever heard before. It was too late. Whatever had been started was in motion. There was no stopping it now.

Marilyn leaped to her feet, dumping Brick to the floor. She fumbled desperately for the amulet and finally drew it from her pocket by its chain. Holding it before her, she looked at it and cried out in horror.

The amulet was looking back at her. A single eye, round and red, seemed to be staring into her very soul.

12

"HELP ME!"

Despite the horror of it, Marilyn couldn't tear her own eyes from the gaze of the eye in the amulet. She had a feeling that the amulet had become a bridge of some kind, between her world and this other place, the place from which the eye was looking at her.

This other place filled her with dread. Something spoke to her through the fiery gaze, spoke without words, lashing into her soul with a message that told of thousands of years of waiting, of sorrow, and of anger.

Dimly she could hear the others calling her name. She tried to answer, but could not force her lips to form the words. Frustration began to boil within her, causing her chest to feel painfully full, as if there were a balloon swelling inside.

Once, when she was five or six, Kyle and Geoff had tied her up while they were playing some stupid game. Being unable to move her arms or legs terrified her, and after only a few seconds she had begun to scream.

She had the same sensation now, only it was worse because there was nothing binding her—nothing but the blazing eye of the amulet. She wanted to scream. She wanted to throw the amulet as far from her as possible. She wanted to grab Kyle by the hand and run from this place, fleeing the terror they had found here.

But she couldn't. She couldn't even move her lips to ask for help. Her breathing had become short and shallow, and her throat felt as though there were a Coke bottle wedged in it.

Then she heard the voice—the same rough voice she had heard before, first speaking through Brick, and then through Zenobia's corpse.

Only now it was whispering.

And it was saying what *she* longed to say.

Help!

The word blossomed in her mind, where none of the others could hear it, and she thought her heart would break, for it sounded like nothing so much as the cry of a lost child.

A teardrop trickled down the amulet.

Help me, whispered the voice in her mind. *Please, help me.*

Marilyn had never heard such sorrow, such longing. It made her think of a warm night the previous summer, when she had been lying in the grass behind her house, staring at the stars, and had suddenly started to weep because she wanted so desperately to reach out and touch them. She had actually raised her hands toward the sky, stretching toward the stars. But they were too far, hopelessly far away. She had felt very small then—small, and trapped, and infinitely sad.

She had felt the way this voice sounded.

Help me, it pleaded again.

And for Marilyn, who was so softhearted she had been known to walk out of her way to avoid stepping on bugs, there was only one possible answer:

"Yes," she whispered. "I'll help you."

A flood of elation seemed to envelop her body. A pleasant warmth surrounded her.

But somewhere in the distance she heard a horrible sound. After a moment she realized it was Kyle, screaming.

"She's on fire! Help her, she's on fire!"

As the words pierced her consciousness, she became more aware of the heat around her.

"Marilyn!"

Zenobia's voice was the final jolt. She tore her gaze from the amulet. Immediately all the screams that had been pent up in her from the time she first saw the eye came tearing out of her, propelled by a new horror.

Her body was surrounded by leaping, crackling flames.

Don't be afraid, whispered the voice in her mind. *I will keep you safe.*

The reassurance did no good. She buried her face in her hands and screamed over and over—until suddenly she realized that, despite the flame, she felt no pain at all.

She was being held in arms of fire, arms that were enclosing her, taking her someplace she had never been before. Someplace where she was desperately needed.

Are you ready? asked the voice.

"Yes," she whispered, before she could even think of what she might be doing.

The sense of heat increased.

Now! cried the voice.

Marilyn felt herself begin to fade.

"Grab her!" cried Zenobia at the same instant.

Marilyn whirled away from the others, saw them spin into the darkness. She felt a hand clutch at her heel. Then everything went black, and it seemed to stay that way for a long, long time.

When Marilyn came to, she found herself lying on a cold, smooth floor. She brought herself to her knees and shook her head, trying to remember what had happened, how she had gotten here.

She looked up. In the distance she could see windows—huge windows, so wide an eagle could fly through them without brushing its wings on either side.

The amulet was still in her hand.

She rolled over and whimpered, pulling her knees against her chest to make herself into a small ball.

Where was she?

She looked up again. How could the windows be so far away? How big was this place?

And *where* was it?

She noticed something and put her hand on the floor, next to her face. The smooth stone beneath her fingers was pitted and scorched, as if something incredibly caustic had fallen upon it.

A cold wind blew over her. She shivered, huddling into herself for warmth.

We're here!

She didn't know if she was glad the voice was still with her or not.

The thought was interrupted by a low moan from somewhere nearby.

She turned in the direction of the sound.

"Kyle!"

He lay sprawled on the floor about ten feet to her left. At the sound of her voice he shook his head and pushed himself to his elbows. A bump the size of a small egg protruded from his forehead.

Raising his fingers, he gingerly touched the lump. "Ouch!" he whispered, making a face. As he did, he seemed to become aware of the room around him. A look of shock crossed his face as he took in the monumental size of the place.

"Where are we?" he asked in a very small voice.

In the Hall of the Kings, replied the voice.

When Kyle made no response, Marilyn realized that the voice was speaking only in her mind. So she repeated the words aloud.

Kyle looked at her. "What's the Hall of the Kings? And how do you know that's what this place is called?"

Marilyn smiled nervously. "A voice in my head told me."

Kyle was still probing at the lump on his forehead. "Are you all right?" he asked, his voice filled with concern.

"No, I'm not all right! I've been attacked by a corpse, swallowed by fire, kidnapped to who knows where by who knows what, and I've got a voice in my head. How can you say 'Are you all right?' I'm going out of my mind!"

"Calm down," said Kyle and the voice in her mind simultaneously.

"I can't stand it!" she screamed. "You! Whatever you are, get out of my head!"

I'm not in your head, answered the voice. *I'm just talking to you that way.*

"Well, why can't I see you?"

I don't think you want to.

"Why not?"

I'm not very pretty.

"I'm not feeling very pretty myself right now," said Marilyn, somewhat irrelevantly.

She received no words in response, only a sense of puzzlement from whatever was talking to her.

"Listen, I don't care *what* you look like. I'd still rather see you if I have to talk to you."

For a moment the voice stayed silent. Marilyn glanced over at Kyle, who was staring at her in astonishment.

"Well?" she cried at last.

I'm afraid, said the voice.

"Of what?" she asked impatiently.

Of frightening you. I need your help, and—

"Look, if you want my help, let me see you!"

You'll scream.

"In about ten seconds I'm going to scream anyway!"

Kyle had crawled over and was sitting beside her. He pressed his hand against the inside of her elbow.

The creature materialized in front of them.

Marilyn began to scream. Kyle shouted in terror. The creature vanished abruptly.

I knew you would scream, said the voice petulantly.

"You killed my aunt Zenobia!" cried Marilyn. "I saw you. I saw you in my dreams! You killed her!"

She could feel his chagrin. *That was an accident. I didn't want her to die. I just wanted her to give the amulet back!*

"You killed her!"

Kyle's arms folded around her.

She felt a stony silence in her mind.

"What was *that?*" asked Kyle at last, his voice a mere whisper. She turned to him. His face was etched with lines of fear, and his eyes were deeply troubled. "What's going on?" he asked, sounding so much like a frightened little boy that she could have wept.

"I don't know. I told the voice in my head I wanted to see it."

Kyle shuddered. "You mean that ... *thing* is what you've been talking to?"

"I guess so. The worst part is, I've seen it before."

"Where?"

"In a dream."

"What did you mean when you said it had killed Zenobia? I thought she died of a heart attack."

"She did. But what *caused* the heart attack was that thing we just saw. It scared her to death." Marilyn paused. "Actually, that's just what I saw in my dream. But it seemed so real, I assumed it was what happened." She gave him a weak smile. "Considering what's going on, I guess it makes as much sense to believe in dreams as anything."

"Yeah, I guess so," said Kyle numbly. He stood to

look around and gave a low whistle. "Where are we, anyway? Yeah, I know—we're in the Hall of the Kings. But what does that mean? And how did we get here?"

"I know how *I* got here," said Marilyn. "That creature brought me." She couldn't suppress a shudder when she thought of it. "What I don't understand is how *you* got here."

"I came with you. When you started to disappear, Zenobia screamed for me to grab you. I lunged for you and just managed to catch your heel before you disappeared completely. The next thing I knew, I was lying on this floor, nursing a goose egg." He shook his head and touched the discolored lump. "I can't believe I used to think you were boring."

"I'm beginning to think boring's not so bad," replied Marilyn.

Kyle stretched out his hand to help her to her feet. Once up, she linked her arm through his and pulled herself close.

Why does this make me feel better? she wondered. *I know there's nothing he could do if that monster decides to attack us.*

She looked up at Kyle, who was studying the room—looking for a way out, she assumed. Almost reluctantly she turned her face from his and followed his gaze. For the first time the full extent of the place sank in on her.

It was enormous.

Kyle gave another low whistle. "I was in the Astrodome once. That was like a family rumpus room compared to this."

They turned in a slow circle. On three sides the

polished stone floor swept away for hundreds of feet before coming to a wall. The walls themselves appeared to be carved with some sort of pictures, though Marilyn couldn't make them out from where she stood. The carvings were separated by high, peaked windows. The only thing Marilyn could see through them was clouds.

The walls soared up some forty or fifty feet before the roof took over and continued the upward swing. Kyle guessed out loud that the arch of the ceiling peaked at about a hundred feet above the center of the hall.

The fourth wall was not far from them. Centered against it was a huge throne, mounted on a platform.

Marilyn swallowed uneasily. "Do you think anyone actually sat in that?" she whispered.

"I don't know. If he did, I sure hope he's not around now."

Taking her hand, he led her up the steps of the platform. The seat of the throne—covered with a plush, scarlet material somewhat like velvet, yet different than anything Marilyn had ever seen, or felt—was about shoulder height.

She shivered. "I wonder where the creature went," she said, glancing behind her. "He said he needed help."

"So do we," replied Kyle. "Come on."

He led her across the hall to one of the windows.

Looking out was dizzying, because the ground was nowhere in sight. Pulling themselves up to lean out over the sill (which was nearly as high as Marilyn's chin) they could discern the outlines of the building they were in. It seemed to be a great fortress or castle of some sort, built on the side of a mountain and situated so high that there were clouds *below* them, obscuring the view.

"If I wasn't so scared, I would think it was beautiful," whispered Marilyn. She slid back to the floor. Resting her arms on the wide sill, she gazed worriedly out at the clouds.

"If I wasn't so scared, I would think I was dead," replied Kyle. "This doesn't look real to me. But I don't think your stomach can have this many knots in it once you've actually kicked the bucket."

A cool breeze riffled through his butter-colored hair. Marilyn shifted against him, and he put his arm around her shoulder. She set the amulet on the sill so they could both look at it. The red jewel in the center was flashing angrily.

"What is this thing?" she asked. "Why has it caused me so much trouble?"

Kyle shrugged. "I don't have the slightest idea what's going on. You haven't been willing to tell me anything about it."

She leaned her head against him. "I just didn't want to drag you into this."

"If we ever get out alive, it will have been worth it."

"Right now, that seems like a big *if.*" She sighed and began to poke at the amulet's chain, spreading it into a golden circle that glittered on the stone sill. Finally she said, "I'll tell you what's happened so far." Speaking quickly, she filled him in on her experiences since the night Zenobia had first come to her with the amulet.

He listened with growing astonishment. When she was done he said, "If you had told me all that before tonight, I would have said you were losing your mind."

"That's one reason I didn't tell you."

He nodded. His eyes were troubled, and he was silent for some time. Finally he said, "So what do we do now?"

"Look for a way out, I guess."

There is no way out! roared the voice in her mind. The suddenness of it caused Marilyn to shriek and jump. As she did, her hand caught against the amulet, shoving it outward so that it slipped over the edge of the sill.

The chain went slithering after it.

With a little scream Marilyn lunged for it.

She was too late. Her fingers closed on thin air. As she watched in horror, the amulet disappeared into the clouds below.

13

ENTER THE DEMON

Marilyn leaned over the sill, staring down at the billowing clouds.

"Now what do we do?" she whispered, half expecting the voice to answer her. But it was gone again.

"I don't know," said Kyle. "I have a terrible feeling that amulet was connected to our chances of getting out of this place." He had his arm around her waist and was leaning over the sill with her. Suddenly he cried, "Look!"

Marilyn saw it, too: a glint of gold in the air below them. Suddenly they could see as well a flash of red through the clouds, like a stray beam of light at sunset.

"It's the amulet!" cried Marilyn.

With the chain dangling behind it, the amulet floated

back to the windowsill. She snatched it almost before it landed.

Now be more careful! said the voice angrily.

"He's back," Marilyn whispered to Kyle. Looking around cautiously, she said out loud, "Who are you?"

My name is Guptas.

"I figured as much. Why did you bring me here?"

I need your help.

"What's he saying?" asked Kyle impatiently.

"He says he needs our help." Turning to address the air in front of her, she said impatiently, "Isn't there any way you can talk to both of us?"

Not unless you can see me. And you can't bear that.

"I can, too," said Marilyn defensively. "I just wasn't expecting you to be . . ."

So ugly? asked the voice bitterly.

She hesitated. That was it, of course, although *ugly* was a rather mild word to describe this creature as far as she was concerned. But there was such a sense of sadness in the question, she hated to answer it honestly.

Don't worry, said the voice. *I'm used to it. Do you really think you are strong enough now?*

"Maybe if you answer a few questions first."

All right.

"Ask it what it is," suggested Kyle.

The voice didn't wait for her to repeat the question. *I'm a demon.*

"He says he's a demon," she whispered to Kyle. She could feel him shudder. Turning her attention back to the voice, she asked, "So you're evil, right?"

Let's say that I am. If so, would you expect me to answer that question honestly?

Marilyn paused for a moment, puzzled by the response. "How can I trust you?" she asked at last.

A howl of rage ricocheted through her head, and a sorrow beyond anything she had ever known pierced her heart.

You can't trust me! screamed the demon. *I am beyond trust. I am Guptas the Betrayer!*

Kyle looked around uneasily, as if he could sense the power of the emotions swirling around him.

Marilyn acted on instinct. Holding the amulet firmly in her hand, she said, "Let me see you!"

At once Guptas shimmered into being in front of them. He looked at Marilyn warily, waiting for her to begin screaming again.

Despite the fact that this time she knew what to expect, Marilyn still drew back in shock. Cringing against Kyle, she could feel him tremble again, which only increased her own fear. Despite that, she was able to hold in the scream that seemed to be beating at the back of her throat.

The creature confronting her was half again as tall as Kyle and more fearful than any nightmare she had ever known. *Any nightmare but one,* she thought, remembering the dream of Zenobia's death.

Thick muscles rippled over a powerful body covered with rough, dark-red scales. A stiff, scaly crest ran down the creature's spine, then on along the fierce-looking tail that lashed restlessly behind it. The tail ended in a spiked point, which looked as though it could skewer a man's chest with very little trouble.

Its hands and feet were armed with four fierce-looking claws. Thick, sharp, and black, they looked like they could slice through thick leather as if it were butter.

But it was the demon's face that made the whole picture at once so frightening yet at the same time strangely bearable. It had a bullet-shaped head, with two horns curving out in a deadly arc over its brow, which beetled forward like a shelf. At the brow's edges perched the beast's ears, which were absurdly tiny—almost cute, thought Marilyn, if you ignored everything else. Nose and mouth thrust outward almost like an ape's; curving fangs thrust up from the lower jaw. The nose itself was nothing more than two slits, ringed with a fringe of rustling membrane.

All that was horrifying enough. But it was the creature's eyes that held Marilyn's attention. They were as she remembered them from her dream: a flickering red and yellow that made you think when you looked into them you were seeing the fires of hell.

But now she saw one more thing when she looked into them: the private hell of Guptas the demon.

They stood staring at one another until the silence seemed to become a living thing between them—the two teenagers locked together at the window, hardly daring to breathe; the demon leaning forward, resting on his knuckles. Guptas shifted his eyes from Kyle to Marilyn and back again, over and over.

Clearly he was looking for something. But for the life of her, Marilyn couldn't figure out what.

When the silence finally became unbearable she asked, "What do you want of me?"

At least, that was what she tried to say. Her throat had become dry, almost sealed on itself, and the words would not come out.

Kyle squeezed her hand, and she tried again.

"What do you want of me?"

"My freedom," replied the creature, speaking aloud now.

There was a tentativeness about the answer, as if there were more he wanted to ask for.

"What else?" she whispered.

Guptas shook his head. "Nothing," he said sadly. "There is nothing else I need that you can give me."

"What do I have to do with your freedom?" she asked, though the answer was already beginning to take form in the back of her mind.

The demon hesitated, and a wary look came into its eyes.

"And why *should* she free you, anyway?" asked Kyle indignantly. "You killed her aunt."

A look of rage crossed Guptas's face. "Silence, you!" he roared as he slashed toward Kyle's face with his ferocious claws.

"Stop!" cried Marilyn, thrusting the amulet out before her.

The demon stopped as if frozen, then relaxed back into its former posture. It glared at Kyle as if it would like to tear his heart out.

"I didn't mean to kill the old woman," it snarled. "She died all on her own. She wasn't supposed to do that."

"It's the amulet," said Marilyn, as if she hadn't heard him. "You want me to free you from the amulet."

Guptas nodded.

"But Kyle's question still makes sense," she continued. "Why should I free you?"

A sly look crossed the demon's face. "Because if you don't, I'll kill you."

"I think you'll kill me if I do," said Marilyn.

Guptas looked taken aback. A strange expression, half anger, half grief, crossed his face. "I have no hope," he said hollowly.

Marilyn thought her heart would break. It was not only the creature's words, or even his tone of voice. Some kind of connection had been forged between them now, and she could sense his emotional state. She felt a sorrow greater than any she had ever known, deeper and more profound, even, than she had felt at Zenobia's death.

"What happened to you?" she whispered. "Where did you come from?"

Suddenly she cried out. The amulet, clutched firmly in her hand, grew blazing hot. Her body arched once, then went rigid in Kyle's arms.

"Marilyn!" he cried. He took her by the shoulders and shook her. "Marilyn, what is it?"

Her eyes were wide open, but they seemed blank and distant. He shook her again.

She didn't respond.

She couldn't.

Guptas was answering her question.

14

GUPTAS THE
BETRAYER

She hadn't moved a step, but everything was different.

She still stood by the window.

She still looked across that vast chamber.

But now the place was alive with color and activity. Banners of scarlet and gold fluttered from the ceiling. Exquisite tapestries covered the walls. Musicians wandered here and there, playing lively songs on instruments she had never seen before.

She reached instinctively for Kyle, but her fingers touched only the cold stone of the sill. He was gone.

A shudder of horror racked her body. She was alone in a room filled with beings unlike any she had ever seen—they were enormous, for one thing—and creatures unlike any she had ever imagined. Some resembled Guptas. Others were as different from him as he was from her.

The room bustled with activity.

Almost everyone seemed happy.

She pressed against the sill, waiting in terror for the moment when they would discover her. She felt a throb of pain and realized she was beating her hands against the stone wall.

"Don't be so frightened," whispered a gravelly voice. "They don't know you're here."

The words came from Guptas, who crouched beside her, tail lashing, eyes blazing.

"Watch," he said bitterly. "Watch, and I will show you the downfall of Guptas the Betrayer."

Suddenly she felt a blast of intense heat. She cried out in pain, then lost consciousness.

When she opened her eyes again, the room seemed exactly the same as before. The great bustle of activity continued. The pleasant babble of voices was the same—though underneath it all she now sensed a deep current of joy and contentment.

But that, she understood, had been there all along. Then she realized the one thing that really was different. Now she was seeing all this *through* the eyes of Guptas.

The sense of heat remained. Not impossible to bear, it hovered on the edge of pain, like a dull toothache never quite out of mind.

"Relax," whispered Guptas.

Mere words could never have convinced her to do so. But she had become linked with Guptas at an even deeper level, and she could sense what was in his mind. Examining it, she could read no ill will toward herself—only a simmering anger directed elsewhere, and a deep, enduring sorrow.

In relation to herself, she could sense only one thought: Guptas was terribly anxious for her to know something.

She relaxed.

A corona of fire blazed before her eyes.

The final barriers vanished, and in a matter of moments, she knew the story of Guptas's life.

Because she was living it.

Marilyn stood next to the king. His hand was resting lightly on her head; together they looked out at the great hall.

Her tail lashed back and forth in amusement. All this belonged to Suleiman.

And she was Suleiman's favorite.

Hundreds of people filled the hall, all of them tall, all of them beautiful.

Beneath their feet, hardly noticed, scampered the demons. Once even a single demon would have been cause for alarm here. But it had been a thousand years since the king had tamed them, a thousand years since the war between the demons and the people of Suleiman had ended.

The race of the Suleimans had triumphed, and peace ruled the castle.

Life was good.

Or it should have been.

She paused. Something was nagging at the back of her mind, some thought that stood in the way of her happiness.

She tried to find it, but could not. It was locked away more securely than Suleiman's books of wisdom.

She looked back out over the throng and tried to regain the sense of pleasure she had felt. It was gone. Her tail continued to lash, but it was in anger now, not contentment. She wanted to drive the spike at its tip through someone's heart. Maybe then she would feel better.

She recoiled from the thought, and suddenly she understood at least part of what drove Guptas. He was a being at war with himself.

A sudden flourish of trumpets caught her attention. The great doors at the end of the hall swung open and the king's son entered, standing astride a great carpet that floated through the air. A shout went up. The hero had returned.

Marilyn felt her heart leap. The prince was her best friend.

She loved him.

She hated him.

Why? she wondered.

The answer formed as quickly as she asked for it: She hated him because he had Suleiman's love, and she wanted that all to herself.

A murmur rose among the demons. The one closest to the throne caught her eye and snickered.

A fist of ice clutched her heart. She was on the verge of doing something terrible.

She didn't want to do it.

And she knew she would not be able to stop herself.

Again the world seemed to spin around her, and again she was somewhere else—seeing, *living* a different scene.

This time it was a cave, dark and foul smelling. A dozen demons crouched around her, urging her to lead them. Not one of them was more than half her size. She was the greatest demon in the court. And she was Suleiman's favorite.

"Help us, Guptas," wheedled a voice next to her. "You owe it to us."

Again she had that sensation of being torn between two loyalties. The demons were her people. The king was her master. Her heart belonged to both. And it was breaking.

"You're waiting for something that will never happen," hissed a voice to her right.

Still she hesitated.

One more voice, sharp and bitter: "Remember what the Suleimans did to our people."

The speaker was a very old demon. He sat directly across from her, crouching between two stalactites that thrust down from the roof of the cave like fangs. Somewhere behind him flickered an evil-looking fire that caused his shadow to stretch toward her like a dark hand.

He rose and walked in her direction, the shadow moving before him. Marilyn cringed, aching to cry out in terror, to run not only from these creatures but also from the horrible thing they were asking her to do.

She reminded herself that she was only an observer, lodged temporarily in Guptas's body to learn the secrets of his past.

The ancient demon was standing directly in front of her now. He took her chin—Guptas's chin—in his withered claws and held it steady. His eyes seemed to be boring into Guptas's head.

For a wild, terrifying moment Marilyn wondered if the old demon knew she was in there.

His face was shriveled and evil, and she felt she was in the presence of a force as old as time, as wicked as hate.

In a low, gravelly whisper, he hissed, "Remember what Suleiman did to your mother!"

Guptas erupted in rage, and Marilyn felt as if her brain was on fire.

What? she cried out in Guptas's mind. *What did he do to her?*

She felt as if a door had slammed in her face as Guptas's mind sealed the answer away from her.

Suddenly the world spun again, and they left the cave behind. Marilyn seethed with frustration. Guptas wanted her to know something, but he wouldn't show her all of it.

Why the sudden shyness? she wondered. *Fear? Sorrow? Shame? What is it that he won't let me see?*

They were back in the Hall of the Kings; Suleiman's son was still riding his flying carpet up the center of the hall in his triumphal parade. The throng that filled the court was shouting joyfully at his entrance.

Suddenly Marilyn was aware of the old demon who had spoken to her in the cave. Though he was standing on the other side of the hall, he was staring into their eyes—her eyes, Guptas's eyes—and speaking directly into their mind.

Remember, he growled. *Remember, and repay!*

The crowd was shouting the prince's name. For a year he had been traveling the land, doing his father's business. He had extended the rule of the Suleimans. He had brought peace to the borders of the kingdom, burnishing the golden age that had begun with the defeat of the demons.

The magic carpet paused before Suleiman's throne, hovering a foot or two above the ground.

The king rose to greet his son.

Slowly, silently, unnoticed in the joyous throng, a dozen demons crept to the edges of the crowd. They positioned themselves near the prince, waiting.

Guptas stood beside the king. From across the hall the ancient demon was burning a message into his brain: *Now, Guptas. The time is right. But they have to move together.*

Guptas didn't move.

The words rang in her head, and Marilyn wanted to cry out for them to stop.

Now! demanded the demon. *All we need is the signal. All we need is your word, Guptas, to begin our revenge for a thousand years of slavery!*

Still Guptas hesitated.

Suddenly a picture flashed in and out of his mind like a streak of lightning. Marilyn was left with only an impression of a woman, a woman vastly beautiful yet somehow evil, at once more and less than human.

Remember!

Guptas looked down at the carpet. Everything was in place.

Remember!

A red haze seemed to float through his mind. Marilyn caught his rage, felt herself aching with anger, longing for revenge.

"Now!" screamed the demon.

"Now!" screamed the girl.

It came out as a single word.

At their signal the demons leaped. Grabbing the front edge of the floating carpet, they rolled it under itself, peeling it back so that the prince was suddenly standing on nothing. When he stumbled and fell to the floor, his body was instantly covered with a mass of writhing demons.

A roar of anger erupted from the king.

The crowd began to scream.

The prince was battling the hordes of demons.

And he was calling Guptas's name, calling to him for help.

Again, Marilyn felt the world whirl sickeningly around her. When she could focus again, she found herself sitting in the shade of an enormous tree. The prince, younger now, almost a child, was sitting next to her and saying, "They don't understand you, Guptas. They think you're like all the others." His voice was sad, burdened by the injustice his friend suffered.

Marilyn felt a sudden warmth. The prince trusted her. Even if no one else did, the prince trusted her. He would speak to Suleiman for her. He would tell the king she could be trusted.

"I will fight for you, Guptas," continued the prince. "Because I believe in you."

The prince was calling her name.

"Guptas! Guptas, fight for me!"

She was back in the castle. The throne room was in chaos; demons were attacking everywhere. The king himself was battling a dozen or more, trying to fight past them so he could help his son.

He could never do it in time. There were too many of them.

The prince's cries were growing weaker.

"Guptas, help me!"

He had trusted her! Again that red haze seemed to settle over her eyes. The heat she had sensed from the time she had been joined with Guptas began to blaze around her. She was on fire, and she didn't care. Death filled the air, but she didn't care.

They had to save the prince!

With a cry of rage she threw herself into the battle. She was Guptas, greatest of the demons. With every slash of her claws some other demon's scales fell to the floor, scattering like handfuls of dropped coins. With every sweep of her tail its deadly spike ripped into some soft underbelly, spilling dark demon blood that hissed and steamed like the rivers of hell.

The demons threw themselves on her, their weight bearing her to the floor. Untrained in battle, Marilyn shrieked in horror. But Guptas knew what to do. Arching his body, he sent the demons flying in all directions, and once more began ripping the creatures away from the prince, away from his friend.

In the end they managed to save the prince.

But it really made no difference.

A thousand years of peace had ended with the signal given by Guptas.

The Demon Wars had begun anew.

Three days later the prince was ambushed and slain by demons who waited outside his sleeping chamber.

Guptas went into hiding.

He had betrayed the Suleimans, betrayed his only friend, by signaling the attack. Then, unable to live with that betrayal, he had turned back to the Suleimans he still loved, betraying his own people in turn.

The demons would curse him throughout eternity.

Now his friend was dead, but the war raged on.

Guptas wanted the demons to win.

He wanted the Suleimans to win.

He wanted to die.

As it turned out, that would be the one punishment denied to him.

Five days later the war was over, and the disaster he had initiated was complete.

Guptas was stunned. The last war between the Suleimans and the demons had gone on for a thousand years. How could it be over in two weeks this time?

The answer was simple. The demons had never been inside the castle before. Now, after a thousand years of serving here, they knew its ins and outs as well as they had known their own winding caves. They fought a war of ambush and sudden death. There were no great clashes of armies after that morning in the Hall of the Kings. There was only lurking, hiding, and ambush.

And death.

Now the demons and the Suleimans were gone, all destroyed in this final cataclysm, which had been unleashed by a single word that should never have been spoken.

A word that had come from his lips.

Guptas wandered the halls, sighing and moaning to himself. The castle was littered with bodies, both Suleiman and demon.

And it was all his fault.

He sat alone in empty rooms, beating his breast

with his claws, pounding the floor in his anger and sorrow and guilt.

Was there no one left alive?

"Yes."

Guptas looked up and cried out in terror.

The king was standing before him.

Suleiman didn't say a word, merely motioned for Guptas to follow him. Meekly the demon walked at his master's heels, back to the Hall of the Kings.

The bodies were all gone, and he wondered vaguely what great magic Suleiman had worked to get rid of them.

The king collapsed onto his throne. Guptas sat with his face averted, ashamed to look at his master. But out of the corner of his eye he could see that the king was pale and exhausted, and that his body had many wounds.

After a while the king began to speak. He told of the war, and how it had been fought. He spoke of the death of his son. And then, in a whisper, he spoke of the final great battle, deep in the bowels of the castle, when he had fought alone, against the remaining demons, finally imprisoning them with a spell so powerful it nearly killed him to cast it.

And at last he spoke of betrayal, and the necessary punishment.

Then, despite Guptas's tears, despite his cries of terror, his pleading, his apologies, his groveling, Suleiman worked his last magic.

With his powers he imprisoned Guptas in an amulet the prince had worn from the day of his birth—cursing him to stay inside it until the day someone trusted him enough to release him.

Carrying the amulet, Suleiman wandered out of his castle and down the mountainside. Then he worked his last great act of magic, shoving the castle and the mountain on which it stood out of the world we know, into another place altogether.

For a time the great king traveled this world, seeking a balm for the pain in his heart—until one day, wandering weak and weary through the deserts of Egypt, he simply toppled forward, crushing the amulet into the sand beneath him. He lay in the blazing sun, sweat pouring from his brow, sand clinging to his skin.

There he died.

And there Guptas stayed, for a time longer than anyone could imagine—stayed until the day Eldred Cooley found the amulet.

15

GUPTAS'S SECRET

Kyle was shaking her.

"Marilyn! Marilyn, are you all right?"

She opened her eyes and looked around. She was back in the Hall of the Kings. Guptas stood nearby, looking at her anxiously.

"Are you all right?" asked Kyle again.

She nodded. "I think so. How long was I out?"

"Only a few seconds. But you had me scared."

"A few seconds! But . . ."

The protest died on her lips. She turned to the demon.

"What do you want from me?"

"Let me go."

"I don't understand."

"Let me go. Free me from the amulet."

"But you're free of it right now."

Guptas shook his head.

"I don't understand," she said. "I mean, there you are—"

While she was speaking, Guptas had raised his arm. Before she could finish her sentence, he lashed out at her with his deadly claws.

"Watch out!" cried Kyle. At the same time he threw himself at Guptas, trying to stop the attack. Marilyn screamed and threw up an arm to protect herself.

Kyle slammed into the demon just as the slashing claws made contact with Marilyn's face.

They passed through her cheek and came out the other side without leaving a scratch. At the same moment Kyle hurtled though the demon's body and ended up sprawling on the floor several feet past him.

"You're a ghost!" cried Marilyn.

Guptas actually smiled, though the effect was more that of a hideous leer. "No, I am not a ghost. But I'm not really here. I'm in the amulet, just as I have been for ten thousand years."

Kyle pushed himself to his knees and shook his head. He had another, smaller lump sprouting next to the first one. "So you're a hologram," he said. Gently he fingered the new protuberance. "Did you really have to give such a convincing demonstration?"

"It's important that you believe me," said Guptas solemnly.

Marilyn crossed to Kyle and helped him to his feet. "I believe you. I just don't understand what I'm supposed to *do* for you. Let's take it step by step."

"I want you to let me out of the amulet."

"You've got to be kidding!" cried Kyle. "You think

she's going to let something like you loose when you're good and safe where you are?"

"She will if either of you ever wants to see your home again," snarled Guptas.

"Don't threaten me!" snapped Marilyn. Holding up the amulet, she added, "I don't want to see you anymore."

Guptas vanished instantly.

"How'd you do that?" asked Kyle in astonishment.

"It's the amulet. I'm pretty sure it controls him. Didn't you notice the other time, when he slashed at you with his claws and I told him to stop? I was holding the amulet then, and he obeyed me instantly."

"He couldn't have hurt me anyway," pointed out Kyle, "since he was only a—what? A mirage? An illusion? What do you call something like that?"

Marilyn shrugged. "I don't have the foggiest. Anyway, the point right now is not what we call him. It's how do we deal with him?"

"I'd say the first thing to do is make him take us home."

She held up the amulet. "Guptas! I want to see you!"

She was expecting his image to materialize in front of them again. Instead, the jewel in the center of the amulet flashed.

She looked at it curiously and found herself looking *into* it.

Red. And walls. Wall after wall of smooth, hard crimson, all at odd angles to one another, all too close together, cramping, crowding, holding . . .

She shuddered. This was Guptas's world. This was

the place where he had been imprisoned for ten thousand years.

And now he wanted to get out.

Suddenly one eye appeared in the center of the jewel, as it had in the funeral home. It glared at her sullenly.

"Don't play games with me," said Marilyn fiercely. "I said, 'Let me see you!'"

The jewel flashed again, and instead of an eye, she saw Guptas, impossibly small, crouched and crowded between the facets of the crimson prison.

"Out here!" she snapped.

At once Guptas stood before them. Glaring at her, he said sullenly, "You'll never rest again."

She blinked nervously. "What do you mean?"

"I mean you can control me with that amulet, but only when you're awake. I will be free at night—not free of the amulet. Oh, no, I'm never free of that. But free to haunt you. You'll see me in your dreams. I'll shape myself out of air and stalk your room. When you open your eyes, I'll be there, crouching at the end of your bed, waiting to pounce.

"You may know I'm not solid.

"You may know I can never hurt you.

"But will you sleep? Night after night with me prowling your room, screaming at you in a voice no one else can hear, cursing you with the anger I've built up over a hundred centuries—will you sleep then?"

He smiled fiendishly. "Or will you lie awake night after night, quivering in your bed, trembling at the wrath of Guptas? Will you grow pale and weary—"

"Oh, shut up!"

Guptas fell silent.

Kyle walked over to where the demon stood and thrust out his hand. It went right through the scaly hide.

"Cool," he muttered.

Guptas glanced at him with contempt. Suddenly he threw himself at Marilyn's feet and clasped his arms around her legs. "I want to be real again!" he cried desperately. "Make me real!"

"Talk about co-dependent," said Kyle.

Even though the demon wasn't actually there, the illusion was so powerful Marilyn found herself trying to keep her balance in his grip.

"Please!" he cried. "Please let me out! I won't be bad. You know I won't! You know why I'm there. I've suffered long enough. Let me out!"

"So you can kill us like you killed her aunt?" sneered Kyle.

"I never did!" shrieked Guptas. "I told you, she died all by herself. She wasn't supposed to do that!" His voice grew sly. "Besides, I did that while I was bound to the amulet. I can do it again, whether she frees me or not. I just send a picture, as I'm doing now. As I'll continue to do."

One look at Marilyn's face and he changed tactics again. "But not to you!" he cried, banging his head on the floor at her feet. "You know my story! You know the truth! Let me out! Let me out! Let me out!"

Marilyn hesitated. Finally she said, "I don't think I could, even if I wanted to."

The demon arched his back and spread his arms and screamed. Marilyn covered her ears. But even with her hands pressed against her skull she could hear his anguished pleas.

"What do you mean? Why can't you free me?"

"Because of the curse the king put on you!"

Instantly he stopped screaming and rose to his knees. "What do you mean?"

"Well, what he said when he put you in there. You're bound there until someone trusts you. I can't just say, 'Oh, come on out, it's okay now!' If I don't *trust* you, it won't work."

"You can trust me!" cried Guptas eagerly. "You know that. You can trust me. I'll even be your servant. I'll fetch and carry for you and always do what you ask and . . ."

Marilyn actually broke out laughing. "What would I do with you if I had you?"

"I'm a very good servant," said Guptas sullenly.

"No, you are not," replied Marilyn sternly. "You betrayed your master before. You would do it again."

"Not if my master was true!" cried Guptas. "What about that? What about that, eh? What about what Suleiman did?"

"What did Suleiman do?" asked Marilyn. "You wouldn't show me. You kept it hidden."

Guptas turned away. "He was cruel."

"That means nothing," said Marilyn. "What did he do? You want me to trust you, but you won't trust me. You won't even tell me the whole story."

Guptas turned back to her.

"If I tell you, will you let me go?"

"If you don't, I won't."

"That's not the same thing!"

"I know that. But it's the best you're going to get. Never mind. I'm getting tired of you anyway. Get ready, Kyle. I'm going to make him take us back now."

"Wait ... wait ... wait ... wait ... wait!" howled Guptas. He was rocking back and forth, clutching his knees.

"Well?"

"All right, I'll tell you."

Marilyn tightened her grip on the amulet and waited expectantly.

Guptas hesitated. He glanced at Kyle, then turned again to Marilyn.

"Suleiman was my father," he said at last.

16

THE LAMIA

The three of them—Marilyn, Kyle, and Guptas the demon—sat in a circle on the floor, their legs crossed Indian fashion, trying to make sense of the story the demon had just told them.

At one point in his tale Marilyn had interrupted to fill in Kyle on her earlier experience of seeming to live part of Guptas's life.

"How did you do that, anyway?" she had asked the demon.

He shrugged. "You asked me a question while you were holding the amulet. That gave me permission to answer it."

"But how did you answer it? Did you just send a picture from your head to mine, or—"

Guptas broke in. "No, you were *there*. I took you

back in time to the reign of the Suleimans. And then I let you merge with me, so you could see my story."

"You mean I was really there—really in the past?"

He smiled and nodded. "Fun, wasn't it?"

She shivered a little.

"Let's get back to the point," said Kyle. "How do we find out if you're telling the truth about your father and this ... what did you call her? A lamia?"

Guptas did a backward somersault and stood on his head. "You can't. You'll just have to take my word for it."

"Can't you show us, like you did before?" asked Marilyn.

"I can't take you back to before my birth. How can I show you things that happened before I was born?"

Taking a guess, Marilyn whispered, "Then show us her death."

Guptas tumbled to the floor. He actually seemed to go pale for a moment. Looking up at her, his eyes filled with misery, he hissed, "No."

"It would make things easier."

"No."

"I could command you."

The demon shrugged. "I won't be responsible for the consequences."

"Which would be ..."

He looked directly into her eyes. She flinched, but did not turn her gaze away. Once again she had the sensation of looking into the fires of hell.

"A memory," he said at last. "A memory you will

carry with you the rest of your life. A nightmare you'll have to live with."

"You've already threatened me with that if I don't free you. I'm stuck in the middle."

"I shouldn't have threatened you before," said Guptas. "I'm sorry."

She looked at him in astonishment. His voice sounded genuinely apologetic.

He read her eyes. "Don't be so surprised! I know right from wrong. You've seen part of my life. You know I'm different from the others. Look at me! I am not a demon! I am Guptas—half Suleiman, half demon, and different from anything or anyone you've ever heard of. Don't judge me by what you think or what you fear or what you've heard! Judge me by what I am!"

"Right now you're hysterical," said Marilyn softly.

Guptas began to laugh—a harsh, coughing sound that was two steps on the far side of pleasant.

"Do you really want the story?"

She nodded.

"Him, too?"

She looked at Kyle. His face was grim. But he nodded.

She held up the amulet. "Tell us both. No tricks."

Guptas looked hurt. "I had no tricks in mind. How do I make you trust me?"

"You don't," said Kyle softly. "You just make it *possible*—by being trustworthy."

Guptas shot him an angry look. "Put your hand on the amulet," he said. "Both of you hold it. And remember . . . you asked for this."

Kyle slid around next to Marilyn and closed his hand over hers.

And they were gone.

Guptas stood cowering behind his father. Suleiman laid a hand on his head to comfort him.

Marilyn relaxed at the touch. The king had the hands of a healer.

Only he wasn't king yet. Guptas aimed some thoughts in her direction, and she understood that what they were about to see predated her last experience in the past. The king she had seen that time was still a prince now. His father was on the throne.

His name was Suleiman, too—as was that of every king who had reigned before him.

Guptas's father wore a short tunic made of black and scarlet cloth embroidered with gold. A band of silk circled his forehead, binding his long jet-black hair. He had a strong nose, olive skin, enormous dark eyes. He was incredibly handsome.

Marilyn felt a surge of emotion. It was coming from Kyle. With a start, she realized it was jealousy.

"Where are we?" he asked.

"In the Hall of the Kings," replied Guptas.

"I know that," he said sharply. "But where in the hall? Where are Marilyn and I?"

"Inside me," said Guptas simply. "Just watch. Both of you."

She watched. The hall was filled, as before. And there was an air of expectancy. But this time it was not joyful. There was fear in it, and horror.

Two guards brought in a woman. A murmur of disgust rippled through the court.

Marilyn cried out at the surge of emotion that ran through Guptas. She felt Suleiman's hand slide down his neck and onto his shoulder, drawing him close. Guptas clung to his leg, which was like a young oak. Suddenly she realized that at the time of this scene Guptas was little more than a babe.

"Twelve hundred years," said Guptas, in answer to her unspoken question. "This is twelve hundred years before the last scene I showed you. The Demon Wars are still raging in their full fury. Suleiman-the-king, he who sits on the throne, has reigned for over eight hundred years. In all that time he has never been able to defeat the demons."

He paused, then added: "Now his son has fathered one."

The woman struggled wildly, until she looked over at Guptas. Then she stopped. Marilyn read a terrible longing in her face.

Whatever else she was, she was beautiful.

It was a wild, terrible beauty—untamed, fascinating, almost frightening.

She was dressed in gossamer rags. Marilyn had the feeling they were the remnant of some once beautiful gown she had destroyed in her fury.

Her hair was fire red, redder even than Marilyn's, something she would never have thought possible.

And her eyes . . .

Her eyes were locked on Guptas now, looking right into him—and at the same time, it seemed, into Marilyn. As in the demon cave, she had the uneasy sensation that perhaps her presence here was not a secret after all.

They were wild eyes, wild and filled with anger. But

there was a softness in them when they gazed on Guptas.

The demon tightened his grip on his father's leg, digging his claws into the flesh.

Prince Suleiman seemed not to notice. His eyes were riveted on his wife. Marilyn felt a tremor run through his body.

The king rose from the throne. He was tall, taller even than the prince, with a great gray beard that flowed over his chest. He wore a thin circle of gold on his brow. His face was deeply troubled.

He went to the woman.

"Behold!" he cried to the court. "Behold, the lamia!"

Reaching out, he grasped her hand.

Marilyn recoiled in horror as the woman dropped her human shape and revealed herself for what she really was.

Her skin blistered over, turning red and scaly. Great peaked wings shot out behind her. Dark claws curved out from her fingertips.

Prince Suleiman flinched. This was the woman he had loved, the mother of his child.

Two guards held her, but it was the power of the king that kept her in check. She writhed in their hands, cursing the king, cursing the race of the Suleimans. Her eyes were like fire. Her tongue, flickering out between blackened lips, was like a cleft snake.

"Will anyone speak in her defense?" asked the king.

The court was silent, a silence that seemed to fill the great hall with a heavy sense of doom.

The lamia wrenched herself around to face the

prince. Her demon shape faded and she was a woman again, soft and desirable. Her eyes pleaded with him.

Prince Suleiman shuddered, but remained silent. Blood trickled down his thigh where his half-demon son was sinking childish claws into the flesh. The prince tightened his grip on the demon child's shoulder.

"Father?" whispered Guptas.

The prince said nothing.

The woman faded, and the lamia reappeared.

They brought in the ice, and she began to scream.

They were back in their own bodies, in the echoingly empty Hall of the Kings.

"What happened?" cried Marilyn. "Why did you bring us back?"

Guptas turned on her in fury.

"Wasn't that enough?" he cried. "Must I watch my own mother be executed a second time just to satisfy your curiosity?"

He strode away from her. "Ice," he whispered. He spun back, and his voice rose to a shout. "They did it with ice! She was a creature of fire, and ice was fatal to her. They brought in a great jagged block of it and slowly pushed her into it. The first bits of it that touched her hissed and melted against her flesh."

He shuddered.

"Her skin began to peel off. She screamed and cried to my father for help. I turned his leg to ribbons with my claws.

"But there was no help for her. No compassion from anyone in that hall—because she was a lamia, a mother of demons, and had tricked the prince into loving her. So they stood in silence as the king's murdering guards pushed her into the ice and her skin sizzled away from her body."

The demon's image walked back and stood before Marilyn. "Do you still wonder," he whispered, his voice intense, harsh with pain, "why I had mixed feelings about my father?"

He paused, then stretched his claws upward and screamed, "Or about myself? Look at me. Look at what they made me! I was the firstborn child of the firstborn child! I have royal blood coursing through my veins! I should have been king. I should have been Suleiman!

"But my father loved a lamia, and then let her die." He turned away and sat huddled into himself.

"That was the beginning of the end of the Demon Wars," he said after a while. "My father fought as no Suleiman ever had before. He led the people into battle, and they were invincible. But I know that with every slash of his sword he was slashing at his own heart. I know his guilt. I know his fury at himself for remaining silent.

"I even understand it! That's the hardest part of all! I can't even condemn him totally. She should never have come to him. She was wrong. He was wrong. Everybody suffered. And in the end I destroyed their world. And my own."

"I'll let you go now," said Marilyn.

Guptas turned to her in astonishment.

"What?"

"I'll let you go now. You've suffered long enough."

He threw himself at her feet. "Thank you!" he cried. "Thank you. Oh, thank you!"

"Stop it!" she said in disgust. "Remember who you are!"

He stood, a strange expression on his face, pride and surprise mingling together.

She lifted the amulet and began to speak.

"Don't!" cried a voice behind her.

She spun around. It was Eldred Cooley. Beside him stood Zenobia. She held Brick in her arms.

"You must not do this," said Cooley sternly.

Guptas howled in despair.

17

JUDGE AND JURY

"**N**ever trust a demon," said Eldred Cooley. He glared at Guptas so fiercely that for a moment Marilyn thought he might actually attack the creature.

Zenobia broke the tension by speaking. "Marilyn, are you and Kyle all right?"

Marilyn nodded. "How did you get here?"

"Brick."

Kyle laughed. "You mean that cat is actually good for something?"

"Cats are good for a great deal more than most people realize," said Cooley sternly. "Their ability to track down demons is one of the reasons they were highly valued in the ancient world. It's interesting," he said, turning to Zenobia. "You would think they would have lost the ability over the last several thousand years, since there was no use for it."

"Stick to the point, Eldred," she replied tartly.

"The point right now," he said, turning back to Marilyn, "is how to dispose of that creature you have gained control of."

"Why can't I just let him go?"

Cooley looked at her incredulously. "Do you really want to release such a monstrosity on the modern world?"

"He's had a difficult life," said Marilyn defensively.

Cooley roared with laughter. "Let him go free and you'll find out what difficult is. How do you know he had a difficult life? Did he tell you? He is a master of lies. I repeat: never trust a demon."

"He didn't tell us," said Kyle. "He showed us."

Zenobia dropped Brick, who strolled over to sniff at Guptas. "What do you mean, he showed you?"

"Well, he took us back in time. . . ."

"He touched your minds!" cried Cooley. "Oh, we've got trouble, Zenobia. Lord only knows what he's done to these two kids. They could be completely under his control."

"No!" shouted Guptas.

The sudden shout caused Brick—who had been trying without success to catch a scent from the demon's image—to jump a foot into the air. When he landed he hissed and arched his back.

"I wouldn't do that to them," said Guptas firmly. He made a little slashing motion at the cat, which scurried over to hide behind Marilyn.

"It is pointless for you to say anything," said Cooley, "since we can't believe a word of it anyway."

"Use your brain, you old fool! What is the curse that was laid on me? I cannot be freed of the amulet until someone trusts me enough to let me out. What good would it do me to put them in my power? I could gain obedience, maybe even acceptance. But never true trust. I could never break the binding that way."

"Don't try to use your persuasive ways on me," said Cooley. "I'm too wise for that."

Guptas made a noise of disgust, then vanished.

"Now see what you've done!" said Marilyn.

Cooley was at her side before she finished speaking. Positioning himself in front of her, he began to stare into her eyes. It reminded Marilyn uncomfortably of the meeting in the cavern, when the old demon had looked at Guptas the same way. She shivered.

"I can't tell for certain," he muttered to Zenobia, who was standing at his side. "But I think she's all right."

"Of course I'm all right!" snapped Marilyn, pushing at his hand. Her arm passed through his, and she suddenly remembered that she was dealing with a ghost.

"This is too much," she said.

Kyle came over, holding the cat. "Where are we, sir?"

Cooley turned to him. "Somewhere at the edge of your world. When the last Suleiman left the castle, he pushed it over some magical border, to move it away from the world we know."

"Then what would it hurt to let Guptas free here? It's not as if we'd be letting him go in the real world."

"Other than the fact that he might kill you instantly, you should be able to see that he can transport himself between our world and this castle with no trouble. He'd be back on earth raising hell in no time flat. No, there is no way around it. He must be destroyed."

"I'll bet you support the death penalty, too," said Kyle, scratching Brick between the ears.

"I won't destroy him," said Marilyn flatly.

"Marilyn, be reasonable," said Zenobia. "He's an evil creature. Look what he did to me!"

"He didn't mean to," said Marilyn uncertainly. "He just wanted you to give him the amulet."

"Why?" cried Cooley, pouncing like a cat that had spotted a mouse. "Why did he want the amulet back?"

"Because I was afraid she might be as much of a fool as you were!" roared Guptas, suddenly reappearing beside them.

Marilyn was sure that if Cooley hadn't been a ghost, he would have gone pale at that moment.

"The owner of the amulet has power over me," continued Guptas. "I don't like that, so I don't want anyone to own the amulet. I don't want anyone to control me. Most of all, I want to be free. But it was clear you had poisoned the woman's mind against me. If I couldn't get her to free me, I wanted at least to be free of her control. I never meant for her to die. I was terrified when her heart gave out. I had had no idea that might happen. You people are much weaker than the Suleimans."

"And me," said Cooley. "What about what you did to me?"

"You," said Guptas simply, "deserved to die. But I didn't do it. It was your own greed that did you in."

"What do you mean?" cried Cooley. "I ordered you to lead me to something valuable in this castle." He stopped and looked around him, then added defensively, "Because I wanted to prove to Zenobia what kind of possibilities I had uncovered."

"You've been here before?" gasped Zenobia.

"Of course. This creature led me to a valuable artifact, all right. But it was a trap. When he took me back to my hotel room and I opened the thing—"

"When you opened it, you found death," said Guptas.

"That's right!" shouted Cooley. He turned to the others. "He admits he tricked me! He showed me a precious box, but inside was some curse of the Suleimans."

Even now, as a spirit, the memory made him shudder. "When I opened the box, a hideous centipede scuttled out. It was a great purplish thing, mottled and twice as long as my hand. It slithered up my sleeve." His eyes grew wide with remembered horror. "It ran up my shirt, and while I was trying to tear open my collar—it bit me."

"It had a very powerful poison," said Guptas softly.

"You see!" screamed Cooley. "I asked him for a treasure, and he gave me death!"

For a moment no one said a word. Then Zenobia began to chuckle.

Guptas smiled. "I see you understand."

Comprehension dawned in Cooley's face. "You tricked me," he repeated bitterly.

"Not at all," said Guptas. "You merely leapt to conclusions. That box was a mere trifle for the Suleimans. The treasure was inside. You asked for something valuable, and I gave you the most precious thing

I could think of, the thing I have longed for for ten thousand years. I gave you death."

Cooley was furious. "Give me that amulet!" he said, snatching at Marilyn's hand. His fingers passed right through hers, and he made a gesture of impatience.

"It's hers by right," said Guptas calmly. "You might take it from her, but it will do you no good. The amulet can be stolen, but its power must pass freely."

"Marilyn," said Cooley, forcing himself to be calm, "please give me the amulet. This creature must be dealt with now."

"No," said Marilyn. Her voice was shaking.

"Now, listen here, young lady—"

"Eldred, shut up!" said Zenobia sharply.

To Marilyn's surprise, Cooley backed off like a whipped dog.

"Marilyn, be reasonable," said Zenobia. "This creature is evil. He is a demon!"

"*Half* demon," said Marilyn.

"Well, that's interesting," said Zenobia, raising a ghostly eyebrow. "But it doesn't make any difference. In his heart he is wicked. And he is powerful. All the time the amulet lay in the desert, the world was safe from him." She glanced at Cooley. "Far better the amulet should have remained there," she said pointedly. "But it didn't. It was brought out into the world. And now it is an unbelievable menace. If you do not free Guptas, somehow, someday, someone else will. And when that happens, I fear the whole world will pay."

She paused for a moment, then touched her niece's cheek with a hand that wasn't really there. Marilyn shivered at the sensation.

"It isn't fair," said Zenobia. "But it has come down to you. You must decide for everyone."

"So I'm judge and jury," said Marilyn softly.

"That's right," said Zenobia. "No matter what El-dred thinks, we cannot force you to make this decision."

"What do *you* think I should do?"

"I'm not certain," said Zenobia. Her face was troubled. "In a way, I could say it makes no difference to me. After all, what happens to the world now is little of my concern. But I don't want to see innocent people suffer."

"Is he so guilty?" asked Marilyn. "He didn't ask to be born. Do you know his story?"

"Do you believe it?" asked Zenobia. "And even if you do, does it make any difference? He is too power-ful—and he is a creature out of time. Once the world could hold him, because there were others with power great enough to keep him in check. But free him now and you unleash an uncontrollable force. There is no one left who can master him, no safe place to put him. He can wreak unimaginable destruction."

Marilyn turned away from her aunt. "Kyle?" she whispered.

Kyle looked at her hopelessly. "I don't know what to tell you. I think Guptas got a bum deal. But I sure don't want him walking the streets of Kennituck Falls at night."

Marilyn went to the window and stared out at the great peaks surrounding them. The air was cool. Glancing down, she could see a break in the clouds, and the ground, incredibly far away. She leaned her head on the sill and tried to think, but her mind was whirling with fear, with anger, with sorrow.

"Why me?" she whispered. "Why do I have to make such a decision?"

The amulet was warm in her hand.

She stood up. "Guptas, I want to see you!"

At once the demon appeared.

"Do you have anything to say?" she asked.

Cooley started to protest. Zenobia cut him off.

Guptas looked around the circle of faces. Marilyn could sense a great weariness in him.

"I have been imprisoned for thousands of years," he said at last. "My world has vanished, and I have no home. I am a slave to whoever holds the amulet."

He turned to Marilyn and looked directly into her eyes. "I want to be free. If you can't free me from the amulet, then free me from life."

He stepped closer to her.

"Let me go, or let me die."

"I thought you couldn't die," she said, her throat tight.

He looked away. His voice little more than a whisper, he said, "There's a way. If you're willing."

18

JOURNEY INTO FEAR

When she thought about it afterward, Marilyn was never certain how much time passed before she spoke again.

She studied the faces around her. Kyle, sweet and gentle, seemed very sad. She wondered what he was thinking. Cooley was fidgeting, chewing his ghostly lips, fighting to keep his mouth shut. Zenobia's eyes were filled with pity. And Guptas looked blank; there was nothing to be read in his face.

Her grip on the amulet tightened until the edges of it were cutting into her hand. She held it pressed against her chest. Closing her eyes, she could feel a tear trickle under her lashes. At last she whispered, "Guptas, I can't do it. I can't free you."

The demon nodded. "So be it."

She opened her eyes. "What do I do now?"

"You kill me."

"I can't do that, either!"

Guptas grinned, a hideous smile filled with fangs. "It's easier than you think. You simply destroy the amulet."

"I tried that," said Zenobia. "Remember?"

He laughed, a harsh, short sound. "I remember. It was pathetic. There is only one way to destroy the amulet, and that is in the forge where it was made."

"Where is that?" asked Marilyn.

"Below us. Deep in the bowels of the castle."

"Make him take us there," said Cooley.

"Shut up!" snapped Zenobia and Marilyn together.

Silence fell over the great hall. Brick came and rubbed against Marilyn's legs. "Will you show me the way?" she asked at last.

Guptas nodded.

Marilyn sighed. "Then let's go."

She couldn't hear it.

She couldn't see it. (Several times, when she thought it was close, she spun around to try, but found nothing.)

Even so, she was certain it was there, following them; some force, some *power* she did not understand.

She had no idea how she knew it was there, but the knowledge of it was driving her to distraction.

"What are you?" she wanted to scream, but resisted, for fear the others would think she was crazy.

They had been walking for hours. At least, it seemed that way to her. With the image of Guptas leading the way, they had left the Hall of the Kings through a secret door behind the throne, entering a world of twisting passages that the demon threaded as if it had been only yesterday when he last walked them.

The sensation of being followed would not go away.

"Do you feel anything strange?" she asked Kyle at one point.

"*Everything* is strange here," he answered.

She gave up and kept to herself what the rational part of her mind insisted was a mere nervous reaction to the insanity that had enveloped them.

She tried to pay attention to the sights around her, telling herself this was a place no other human eyes had ever seen.

It was strange, but strangely beautiful—all out of proportion to her senses, the doors and ceilings built for the great race of the Suleimans. But it was in perfect condition, as if not a moment had passed from the day Guptas's father had sealed the place and left it to the ages. She saw no decay, no dust. The strange carvings in the doorsills were without nicks or chips. The floors in the winding halls gleamed as if they had been polished yesterday.

Each room and corridor had been treated as if it were a work of art. Even as they penetrated deep into the hidden heart of the castle, they found breathtaking tapestries adorning the walls.

She lost count of the rooms they passed. Once in a while Guptas stopped to point through a door, saying, "That's where the king came to be alone" or "This was where they sent me to be punished when I was little."

Marilyn began to have an odd sense of the demon's

life, of a quiet domesticity that seemed oddly incongruous for such a creature.

As they went deeper into the castle, they left the bright areas behind. Here there were no more windows—only strange glowing stones set in the ceiling, stones that cast an eerie light over the halls through which they wandered.

Guptas's comments on the rooms grew stranger: "Here is where the king met his wizards. Here is where the demons came to perform their ceremonies."

"Ceremonies?" asked Zenobia, ever curious.

"I cannot speak of them," he replied.

"How do we know he won't lead us into some kind of trap?" Zenobia had asked earlier.

"That's simple enough," Cooley had said. "Marilyn can compel him to lead us safely. Remember, he is still bound by the amulet."

"He'll lead us safely," said Marilyn.

The moment the words left her mouth, she caught her breath and wondered what would happen: Without intending to, she had shown some trust in Guptas. Would that be enough to release him?

She waited nervously, but nothing seemed to change.

She began to wonder what was happening inside her. How much did she believe in the ancient demon after all? Would her emotions betray her and free him against her will?

She wished they would reach the forge.

And then what, Sparks? Can you really destroy the amulet, knowing that it will mean killing Guptas? You know that demon better than you've ever known any living creature. You've been inside his mind. You've experienced his life. You've felt his pain.

Can you really destroy him?

She backed away from the question. It was too much for her to deal with at the moment.

The sense that something was following them increased. She reached up to stroke Brick, who was riding on her shoulders. The cat's black-and-white tail flicked back and forth.

Ahead of her Guptas stopped. His tail lashed warily from side to side, much like the cat's.

"What is it?" she asked.

"I'm not certain," he growled. He turned restlessly, a worried look on his face. "I sense dan—"

Before he could finish, the floor gave way beneath her.

Marilyn screamed. She felt a ripping sensation on her shoulders and realized, in some corner of her mind, that it came from Brick's claws. The cat had jumped away, using her as a launching pad.

She hit something solid, and all the breath was knocked out of her.

Forced into silence, as soon as she caught her breath she began to scream again, because she was in a darkness deeper than anything she had ever experienced. It was as if something had swallowed the sun, had swallowed all the light that ever existed.

"Be quiet!" snapped Guptas.

"I can't stand the dark!" she sobbed.

He turned on a light. She didn't know how he did it, but she almost wished he hadn't, because the first thing she saw was so horrible it made Guptas look almost pretty by comparison.

The monster sat in a corner. It was obscenely bloated, a dripping mound of flesh with an almost human face and a score of scaly tentacles sprouting from its body. It blinked for a moment when Guptas turned on the light. Then it began to smile.

Welcome, it whispered in her mind.

Marilyn began to inch away.

Oh, don't do that! I'm very hungry. It chuckled softly—a bubbling, slimy sound that made her skin crawl. *I've been waiting a long, long time for someone to step into my little trap.*

As it spoke, a tentacle slithered across the floor and wrapped around her leg. At its touch, her skin began to burn. An odor of death rose from the tentacle's slimy casing.

"Let her go!" roared Guptas.

Her attacker shrank back against the wall for a moment, then sent another tentacle lashing out to wrap around the demon. It made a loop about Guptas. But closed in on itself, passing through the illusion of the demon's presence.

Marilyn beat at the tentacle that held her leg. She could feel blisters erupt on her hand where she struck it. The creature only tightened its grip.

Suddenly she heard a clattering noise. A small cloud of dust erupted to her right. When it cleared she saw Kyle standing near her, looking slightly dazed. He looked around, and the blood drained from his face.

The creature struck out at him. Kyle jumped, avoiding the tentacle, and grabbed a shard of the broken floor that littered the area around them. He slashed at the tentacle that held Marilyn, severing it with one stroke.

The creature howled in rage. The severed tentacle began spurting a green fluid that fell in steaming gouts around her.

"Marilyn, get out of here!" yelled Kyle.

A dozen tentacles shot toward him. But the creature was confused, disoriented by its pain, and Kyle was able to jump away from the attack.

"I'll hold him off!" he shouted. "You get out!"

"Follow me!" cried Guptas, racing past Marilyn. She scrambled to her feet, but looked back when she heard Kyle cry out in pain.

The creature had managed to snare him with one of its tentacles. Now several other tentacles were snaking in his direction.

Though Kyle was screaming, he was still fighting, slashing with the piece of flooring at the tentacle that held him. Each time he struck at the monster it gasped, its cries merging with Kyle's screams in horrible chords of anguish.

"Wait!" Marilyn cried to Guptas. "Wait!"

Guptas stopped. She dashed back and stomped as hard as she could on the tentacle that was holding Kyle. The sickening squashiness beneath her heel made her stomach lurch. The creature shrieked, but loosened its grip on Kyle, who pulled himself free and scrambled backward.

"Come on!" She grabbed him by the hand and they raced after Guptas.

Behind them the creature howled in rage, thrashing its tentacles, one of which reached far enough to lash against the back of Marilyn's leg.

The burning pain spurred her to even greater speed. Letting go of Kyle's hand, she ran on, gasping and panting, every breath cutting into her like a sword of fire. Following Guptas, she raced through tunnels that led to other tunnels, and tunnels beyond that.

Finally, unable to go a step farther, she collapsed against a wall, gasping for breath.

With a jolt, she realized the strange, unseen presence she had sensed earlier was still with them.

What was it?

Seeking comfort, she reached for Kyle's hand, then cried out in horror.

He was gone.

She called his name over and over, but there was no answer.

Turning her face to the wall, she began to sob.

19

SULEIMAN'S FORGE

"Guptas! Where are we?"

The demon shook his head. "I'm not certain."

"What do you mean? This is your home!"

"Of course. But there are miles and miles of corridors and tunnels beneath the castle. Unless you have some kind of landmark, or have been following a pattern, when you get to the lower levels there is no way to tell one place from another."

She looked at him suspiciously. "Did you go get us lost on purpose?"

An evil smile crept over the demon's face. "Free me and I'll take you back to the others."

"I can command you to take me back!"

"It won't do you any good," he said sadly. "I don't know the way."

She looked confused. "Then why did you just say you could do it?"

He shrugged. "It was worth a try."

"Trying to trick me like that won't do much to prove you're trustworthy!" she said angrily.

"What difference does it make now?" he shouted back. "Why should I be trustworthy when you're going to destroy me?"

"It was what you wanted," said Marilyn, feeling guilty.

"I would have preferred freedom."

"I would have preferred never knowing you. I guess we can't have everything." She turned in a circle, then muttered, "What do I do now?"

"I don't know."

"I was talking to myself!"

The demon made a face and disappeared.

"Guptas! Get back out here!"

He reappeared, looking sullen. *Better watch it, Sparks,* she thought to herself. *When you're trapped in the bottom of an ancient castle with a demon, you don't want to make an enemy out of him. Better to have a friend.*

Which raised a question:

"You tried to save me from that creature," she said. "Why?"

Guptas turned away from her. "I like you."

She began to laugh. "You want to know something weird? I'm starting to like you, too."

The corridors seemed to wind endlessly through the dark. Unlike the upper floors, there were no glowing stones here to light the way. The only illumination came from some small magic Guptas worked in order to keep Marilyn from total panic, causing himself to glow enough that he could light the way for them.

The sense of some presence hovering near them remained strong within her.

Marilyn wondered where the others were. Was Kyle lost, too—without even a demon to guide him?

"What was that thing that tried to kill us?" she asked once as they wandered along a particularly winding corridor.

Guptas shrugged. "A mistake of some kind. The Suleimans used to experiment with magic quite a bit. They made a lot of wonderful things, and many others better left unthought of. That thing was undoubtedly some wizard's work that escaped and was lurking here in the tunnels years before my father sealed the castle. Some of those things exist only to eat. They just sleep until something edible shows up. They can last for centuries that way." He thought for a moment, then added, "Or it might have been a punishment of some kind."

"A punishment for us?"

"No. For whoever that used to be."

Marilyn shuddered, and decided not to ask for details.

They had passed through several more tunnels when Guptas gave a cry of triumph. He had led them into a chamber where several passages came together. The floor of the chamber was carved with various symbols, and Guptas had knelt to examine them.

"I've got it!" he said triumphantly. "I can get us to the forge!"

"That's good," said Marilyn in a small voice. She was bone weary. Her shoulder ached where Brick had scratched it, and the places where the monster's tentacles had seared her skin were blistered and throbbing with pain.

Even with all that, she could have gone on. But the final horror had just sunk in: When they reached the forge, she would have to destroy Guptas. And once she had done that (if she *could* do it), she would be all alone, in the bowels of the castle, in the final darkness.

Unless by some miracle the others could find her, she and Guptas would die together.

The first thing they noticed was the smell. It reminded Marilyn of the air after a thunderstorm. Guptas said it was the smell of power.

Then they heard the dull roar of it. Soon the corridor was no longer cool, the stones Marilyn lay her hand against no longer moist.

Ahead they could see a flicker of light.

"Come on!" cried Guptas. "This is it!"

He raced along the corridor, almost scampering in his glee.

"Wait!" called Marilyn, who was far too tired for scampering.

Guptas turned and waited, shifting impatiently from one foot to the other.

"I don't understand," said Marilyn. "Why are you in such a hurry to get here?"

"This was my father's special place."

The demon's smile faded, yet his face looked serene. "This is where he came to work—and to be alone. But sometimes he brought me with him." Guptas was looking in her direction, but she could tell he was lost in his memories, seeing a better time. "Those were the best days for me. When we were in court, or with other people, I was his shame, his embarrassment. He only kept me at his side then for two reasons."

Guptas fell silent.

"What were the reasons?" asked Marilyn gently.

"One was his sense of responsibility. The fact that I existed appalled him. But he would not deny it, nor hide from it. He accepted the burden of his mistake."

"And the other?"

Guptas sighed. "I was a warning against pride. By keeping me at his side, he was faced every moment with the fact of his own imperfection.

"But down here it was different. In the court, in the castle, people tolerated me, grudgingly, as the king's offspring, whatever I was. They tolerated me because they had to. But my demon blood disgusted them, and I knew that.

"My father would never show that he cared for me in front of them. But when he brought me down here, when he came to work, then he would talk to me like a son, telling me things I needed to know, and things that he thought." Guptas turned away. "He treated me as if I were ... human."

To her astonishment, Marilyn realized that Guptas's shoulders were shaking, as if he was weeping. She felt an urge to reach out to the demon, hold him for just a moment and tell him it was all right.

But she knew that if she tried, her arms would pass right through him.

He turned and walked toward the light.

A moment later, when they entered the forging area, they both cried out in astonishment.

"So, this was how it ended," murmured Guptas.

Marilyn wondered vaguely what he meant, but was too caught up in examining the room to ask.

The place was huge. Not as big as the Hall of the Kings, of course, but larger than any other room of her experience.

In the center was a pit of fire, surrounded by a stone rim a little higher than her waist. It was at least twenty feet across, filled with dancing flames of all colors. They seemed to operate on a cycle, flickering softly about three feet higher than the rim for a few moments, then roaring some twenty feet into the air, casting out a surge of heat and light that reached the farthest corners of the chamber.

Stone tables as tall as her head were arranged around the forge, littered with tools and scraps of metal. Other tools dangled from the ceiling, far beyond her reach, but just right, she assumed, for a Suleiman.

She found something attractive, almost seductive, about the flames. She felt an urge to run to them, thrust her hands among them, even fling herself into the pit. She shook herself and forced her eyes away from the forge.

She cried out in horror. A demon was about to attack her! Almost instantly she realized what it really was, and felt silly. The ebb and surge of the flames was casting strange shadows around the chamber. What she had seen, feared, was merely a statue—cleverly wrought, but a statue nonetheless—of a demon on the attack. Its face was contorted with rage. It held a deadly looking ax above its head, ready to strike. The flicker of the flames almost made it seem alive.

She crossed tentatively to it and reached out her hand.

"Amazing, isn't it?" asked Guptas. She jumped, and drew her hand back.

"You scared me." She turned to him. Looking past him, she noticed that the room was filled with the statues. "These are fantastic. Did your father make them?"

"You might say that."

"What do you mean?"

"They aren't statues, if that's what you're thinking."

An explanation began to nag at Marilyn's brain, but she fought to ignore it.

"What are they?" she asked warily, hoping the idea she was not able to press back was wrong.

"Demons," replied Guptas. "My other people." He looked around. "This is where my father fought his last battle. It makes sense. He could have lured them to the forge—for there were things they wanted from him that he kept here. Then when he got them here, he used his power to turn them into stone." Guptas stroked the stone demon with his claws. "It's not an easy spell. I imagine doing this roomful almost killed him."

His voice held a strange tone that made Marilyn uneasy. She began to edge away from him.

"It's an odd spell," he continued. His voice was

crafty now, and his tail was twitching nervously. "Father told me about it once."

"Guptas?"

"Difficult to cast, but not hard to break."

The demon turned to her. His eyes glittering with evil, he asked, "How would you like to meet my family?"

20

NOW LET

DESTRUCTION

REIGN

Marilyn felt her insides lurch. "You wouldn't," she whispered in horror.

Guptas caressed the stone demon with his claws. He had a faraway look in his eyes. "Why not?"

"Because you're not that way."

He crossed to another statue. The light still cast by his body caused the hideous features to spring out of the darkness. They made Marilyn shudder.

Guptas seemed to consider her statement for a moment. "I think maybe I *am* that way," he said at last.

"But they were wicked!"

"I am, too."

"No! I don't believe that."

He pounced on the statement. "Then why won't you free me from the amulet?"

She felt as if she had been struck dumb. She could think of no reasonable answer for his question.

"I don't know," she said at last. "Maybe it's because you scare me."

A momentary look of sorrow crossed his face. "I scare everyone," he said. "So I must be wicked."

"No! No, you can't say that. People just aren't ... aren't used to something like you. They're afraid of what they don't know."

Guptas looked at her. The flicker in his eyes seemed to match the flames in Suleiman's forge, as if they were somehow connected. "I'm afraid, Marilyn. It's been ten thousand years. And now you're going to destroy me. Do you think I'm not afraid? Do you think I don't wonder what will happen next? My father had a soul. My mother didn't. What about me? What will happen to me when you throw that amulet into the forge? Will I be gone forever? Will I meet my father again?" He looked at her with haunted, burning eyes. "Or will I roast in some forgotten hell?"

He reached out for her. "Can you tell me, Marilyn? Can you tell me what happens next?"

The amulet seemed to be burning in her hand. She glanced at it. The red stone in its center was flickering in unison with Suleiman's forge, with Guptas's eyes.

She shook her head. "I don't know," she whispered. "I don't know anything anymore."

Guptas sighed. In the silence that followed, Marilyn again sensed that other presence, watching, waiting. The rhythmic flare of the forge spread eerie colors and dancing shadows through the room, smearing the floor, the walls, the frozen demons with shades of fire and darkness.

She felt as though she were being crushed, as if the great mountain they had wound their way into was slowly grinding her to dust.

Something warm and soft rubbed against her leg, and she leaped to her feet, screaming.

It was Brick.

Kyle came racing into the room. "Thank goodness we found you! I thought you were gone for good!"

Zenobia and Eldred Cooley shimmered into sight behind him.

"How did you get here?" asked Marilyn.

"We found Kyle wandering in the tunnels just beyond where you fell," said Zenobia. "Then Brick brought us here. As Eldred told you, a cat can sense demons."

Marilyn was in Kyle's arms, leaning against his chest, feeling safe for the first time since they tumbled through the floor. "I thought I had lost you," he whispered. "I was terrified."

The peaceful moment ended abruptly.

"What is that creature doing here?" demanded Cooley. "Why haven't you destroyed him yet? Are you insane?"

"I don't—"

Those words were all she could get out. Guptas was on his feet, roaring with anger.

"That's enough! You're right, Eldred Cooley. Never trust a demon! I'll be what you want! I'll prove you're right! But you and your people will be the ones to pay. Because my family and I will pursue you, even beyond the grave. We'll terrorize the living, and we'll haunt the dead. And it will be on your head, Cooley. You are the one who drove me to this."

"Your family!" Cooley laughed. The laugh died on his lips as he looked around the room and realized what the shapes scattered across the floor really were.

Guptas had leaped to the edge of the forge. Standing on the stone rim, he raised his arms and began to speak. The flames shot up behind him, stretching to twice the height they had reached before, responding to the power and the magic now unleashed.

Light the color of blood filled the room. The statues sprang out in hideous detail—dozens of raging creatures, intent on death and destruction.

"*Karra Nakken Re-Suleiman Karras!*" roared Guptas.

The flames surged behind him. He threw back his head and roared with laughter, raising his great claws to the ceiling. "KARRA NAKKEN RE-SULEIMAN KARRAS!"

"Stop him!" cried Cooley. "Stop him! If he frees them now, they could destroy the world!"

"Marilyn!" cried Kyle, shaking her. "Marilyn, use the amulet!"

Marilyn shook her head as if she were coming out of a daze. The amulet was pulsing in her hand, throbbing with power. She held it up; light and fire seemed to drip along her forearm.

"Guptas!" she cried. "By this amulet, I command you to stop!"

The last words were buried by a sound like stone grinding on stone, and her heart sank.

She was too late.

Turning in the direction of the sound, she saw that the demon nearest them was changing. Cracks ran over its surface. A reddish tint began to replace the gray of stone.

Slowly it began to twist its head in their direction. More cracks appeared, then vanished as stone turned to flesh. Most horrible of all, the dead stone eyes glazed over, seemed to shatter like breaking glass, then blazed into life—flickering with the fire of the forge, the fire of the amulet.

The sound of stone on stone was repeated all around them. A guttural murmur of some ancient, forbidden language finding tongue again began to fill the hall.

"Look out!" cried Zenobia as the demon nearest them lunged forward, slashing at them with its ax.

Kyle and Marilyn leaped away, but not fast enough. The blade slashed across the side of her leg, laying it open to the bone, then sank into the floor behind her. As she screamed in pain and shock, the creature struggled to free its weapon so it could strike again.

An angry screech sliced the air behind her. She knew that sound. It was Brick!

She turned in time to see the cat plucked from the floor by one of the demons. Writhing in its grasp, Brick lashed out with one claw and tore open the creature's eye. It split with a hissing sound and liquid fire began to pour down the demon's cheek. Furious, it threw Brick aside. The cat struck the wall and slid to the floor, senseless.

Then Marilyn could see no more, because Kyle flung her to the floor, too. Holding her tight against him, he rolled under the biggest of the stone tables.

They were barely beneath it when a curved blade slashed against the top, cutting right into the stone.

Suddenly an evil face appeared below the edge of the table. A wicked smile split its hideous features.

Another appeared beside it, and then another.

Kyle and Marilyn huddled together and pulled back from the edge. They heard a hissing behind them. Turning, she saw two more of the creatures peering in at them from that side.

"Put your back to mine!" said Kyle. "Get as close to me as you can."

Another face appeared at the end of the table, and a scaly hand reached in for them.

A demon grabbed her arm from the other side. She smashed its hand with the amulet. The demon let go, screaming in agony. Her scream mingled with his, seeming to fill the room.

Marilyn continued screaming. This was no mirage, like Guptas. These creatures were real, and out for blood.

The sound of Kyle crying out behind her brought her to her senses. Turning, she saw that one of the demons had grabbed his ankle and was pulling him from under the table. Marilyn wrapped her arms around him and found herself engaged in a desperate tug-of-war.

A pair of scaly hands wrapped about her leg and began dragging her in the opposite direction. Another pair grabbed her other leg. Her grip on Kyle was slipping. He was screaming now, too, as a dozen evil faces glared in at them, fire in their eyes, steaming saliva dripping from their hungry mouths.

Suddenly Guptas was there, roaring in anger. "Let her go! Let her go!" he cried, slashing out at the demons.

It did no good. His arms, mere illusions, passed through them like moonlight through glass.

"I didn't mean to do it!" he moaned, his voice thick with sorrow and remorse. "I didn't mean to do it!"

A vicious wrench at her legs tore Marilyn's hands from Kyle, and she found herself in the open, outside the table. Somewhere behind her she could hear Kyle screaming.

"The amulet!" cried Guptas. "Use the amulet!"

Marilyn wrenched her hand free of the demon that was holding it. The amulet blazed with light.

"Stop!" she cried.

The demons drew back a bit.

"Stop!" she repeated.

An angry murmur rose from the horde. A set of claws slashed at her arm but missed, as if their owner didn't dare actually strike her.

"Stop!" she commanded a third time, scrambling to her feet as she did.

The demons drew back, forming a wary circle around her.

Kyle was still screaming. With a shout Marilyn broke through the circle of demons. Another circle had formed at the other end of the table. She thrust her way into it, holding the amulet before her like a shield.

Kyle, bleeding in a dozen places, looked up at her. His eyes were glazed with terror.

"Let go of him!" she screamed.

The amulet blazed, grew so hot she almost dropped it, and the demons pulled back.

She reached down to Kyle, still holding the amulet

before her, turning warily this way and that to keep the crowd of demons at bay.

He took her hand and staggered to his feet.

The demons grouped themselves around the two teens, muttering nervously, angrily.

Marilyn could feel herself connected with the amulet, feel the flow of her strength into it, and through it. Though it was holding the creatures at bay, it was draining her as it did. She knew she wouldn't last much longer.

As if sensing this, the demons began to press forward.

Holding the amulet above her, as a lone traveler might hold a torch to ward off wolves, Marilyn backed warily away from them.

They pressed slowly forward, seeming to push against some invisible wall she was creating.

Her heart was pounding against her ribs like some caged animal. The wound on her leg was throbbing, and she was still losing blood. Her head felt light. She feared she was about to faint. But she knew if she faltered for even a moment, she and Kyle were dead.

She felt something against her back, and realized it was the rim of the forge. Together, without speaking, they slid up onto it.

The flames behind them seared their backs.

There was nowhere left to go.

The demons drew closer.

"Marilyn!" cried Guptas. "You can't hold them off much longer. Free me! Free me and I will fight for you!"

"Don't be insane!" shrieked Cooley. "If you let him

loose now, it's the end of everything! He's their leader. They'll be invincible."

The demon horde inched forward. Marilyn could feel her control weakening. The flames roaring behind her seemed to be sapping her strength. Her head was throbbing. She couldn't think.

"Let me out!" cried Guptas again. "Marilyn, let me fight for you!"

Marilyn looked at the demon, then at Cooley. Between them the demon horde, held barely in check by her waning strength, muttered and crouched, waiting to leap, eager to tear her to shreds.

I'm ready to die, she thought. But then she felt Kyle beside her, his arms around her. She couldn't think about his death. She couldn't let that happen.

Her head spun with exhaustion. She staggered and almost fell backward into the flames. It was only a matter of moments before she would lose her grip and the horde would attack.

"Hold on, Marilyn," whispered Kyle, tightening his grip and trying to steady her. "Hold on!"

It wasn't enough. The demons were beating down her resistance. Each of them had its fiery eyes boring into her, willing her to die. They began to chant, some guttural cry that had no meaning but seemed to beat the little remaining strength out of her brain.

She could feel herself wavering.

"Now, Marilyn!" cried Guptas. "Free me now before it's too late!"

The demons were winning. Binding them was like trying to hold water in a sieve.

The chant grew louder. One of the demons made a sudden push forward. Another followed him.

She was losing control.

"Now!" cried Guptas.

"Don't be a fool!" screamed Cooley. "He'll kill you first!"

She stepped back and almost slipped over the rim of the forge. An image burst into her head: Guptas, explaining why he had defended her from the creature in the tunnel. His words whispered again in her mind: *I like you.*

Her grip on the amulet tightened.

"I trust you," she whispered. "Guptas, I trust you. Come forth and protect me."

The demons screamed and lunged forward.

The flames roared up behind her.

She collapsed into Kyle's arms.

And as they struggled to keep their balance on the edge of the inferno, Guptas, the son of Suleiman, returned to the flesh for the first time in ten thousand years.

21

THE HANDS OF
THE KING

Marilyn lost her balance and pitched forward, dragging Kyle with her. They struck the floor and were immediately engulfed by a wave of attacking demons.

Shrieking, crying, clawing, the monsters piled on the two teenagers like sharks in a feeding frenzy.

Marilyn, barely conscious, was aware of their claws tearing at her skin. At the same time she sensed that the creatures were, by their very numbers, slowed in their intent to kill her and Kyle immediately.

The confusion bought them only a few seconds of life.

Those few seconds were enough. Beyond the babble of the demons, she could hear a deep-throated roar, a cry of rage tempered by a strange joy.

Then she felt the demons being pulled away

from her, lifted and flung into the air like scraps of paper.

Guptas appeared above them, his face contorted with a fierce ecstasy.

"Ten thousand years!" he cried. "Ten thousand years, and finally free!"

He grabbed a demon in each hand and smashed their skulls together, then flung them forward into the forge.

The flames roared explosively, shot up, and scorched the ceiling as the cries of the dying demons filled the room.

Guptas's tail swept behind him, knocking the demons off their feet.

"It was you!" he cried. "You! I listened to you, I helped you, and everything went wrong! Never again! Never again!"

He lashed out, his great arms sending the smaller demons flying to the right and left. Marilyn and Kyle edged away from the fray. Suddenly Zenobia was at their side.

"Over there," she whispered, pointing to a fallen table. "You'll be safer there."

They scurried along the side of the forge and scrambled behind the table.

On the other side they could hear the battle raging. Unable to resist, they peered over the edge and cried out in despair.

Guptas, larger and stronger than any of the others, had had the advantage when he attacked them. But now their sheer numbers were working against him. They were attacking from all sides, climbing on his back, pulling at his legs, slashing at him with whatever weapons they could lay their hands on.

"Off!" he roared, tearing them from his body and sending them flying into the forge.

The flames were soaring, eagerly devouring every demon that landed in their midst.

"Guptas!"

The voice that rang out was strong and powerful. The fighting stopped. Marilyn cried out in horror and surprise.

It was the old demon—the one who had urged Guptas to give the signal for the rebellion in the Hall of the Kings. Though cracked with age, his voice was powerful, commanding.

"Guptas, stop this foolishness. You are one of us. Destroy those meddling children. Then lead us back to the world. To the *world*. You are the greatest among us. You can be our king. Guptas, lead us to the world again!"

"Don't listen to him," whispered Marilyn. "Guptas, don't listen to him!"

The old demon had locked eyes with Guptas. "Be our king," he whispered. "Don't be a fool. Don't betray us. There is no place for you but with us, no friends for you but us, no hope for you but us. Destroy them, and take your place as our king!"

Guptas stood as if entranced.

"Guptas!" cried the demon nearest him. "Guptas the king!"

The others took up the chant. "Guptas the king! Guptas the king!"

"You were born to rule!" cried the old demon. "Your mother was a queen among demons. Your father was king of the Suleimans. There was never another like you. There was never another Guptas! You will be greater than any king that ever reigned. The world will be yours!"

"You see!" shrieked Cooley. "You see what will happen, you young fool? You've given him the world!"

"Eldred, shut up!" said Zenobia.

"King of the world," whispered Guptas.

Marilyn dragged herself from behind the table. "Don't listen to him," she begged. "Guptas, don't listen to him!" She staggered toward him. "Guptas, don't betray me!"

The demon closest to her grabbed her about the waist. Snarling with fury, he dragged her toward the forge. His claws tore into her flesh.

"Guptas!" she screamed. "Save me!"

The demon had her at the rim. She could feel the heat and fury of the flames as her captor lifted her over the edge.

Kyle started for the forge and was immediately tackled by a dozen demons. He hit the floor with a bone-jarring crash.

"Guptas!" he cried desperately. "Fight for her!"

Marilyn beat at the scaly back of the demon clutching her. "Guptas!" she screamed. "Guptas, I need you!"

Her tears fell to the rim of the forge, sizzling instantly into steam. "Guptas!" She was weeping now as much for him as for herself. "Guptas, I trusted you! Fight for me!"

The demon who held her, small but powerful, raised her above his head. She clung to his hard arms, screaming in terror, as he tried to throw her into the flames.

Guptas began to roar. It started deep in his throat and came rumbling up like a volcano erupting, until his anger shook the very walls around them.

"Let her go!" he roared, at the same moment launching himself through the air to grab her from the demon's arms. "Let . . . her . . . GO!"

He wrenched Marilyn free, tucked her safely under one arm, and with the other picked up the demon and threw it into the forge.

The flames roared gratefully.

"Back!" cried Guptas. "Back, all of you!"

"Destroy the traitor!" cried the old demon. "Guptas must die!"

With a cry of rage the demons surged forward. Guptas placed Marilyn behind him, against the wall of the forge, and stood to guard her against the onslaught. But their numbers were too great. Though demon after demon went sailing over his shoulder and into the flames, it seemed there were always more coming. Guptas was bleeding from a dozen places, and then a dozen more. His sizzling black blood etched its way into the floor.

He was staggering, weakening from the punishment.

And then, so suddenly it was a shock, the demons were gone.

All but one. The old demon who had urged Guptas into his first betrayal.

"Traitor!" hissed the demon. "Fool! What will you gain for this? Nothing!"

He spat in Guptas's face.

Guptas reached forward.

"My grandfather," he whispered. "Father of my mother, king of lies, agent of hate, maker of war. I have waited too long to kill you."

"You never will," sneered the old demon.

"You are wrong," said Guptas simply. "The time has come for you to pay at last. It was all your fault, wasn't it? Everything that happened from the moment you urged my mother to deceive the king. The lies, the betrayal, the destruction—all of it is on your shoulders."

He reached forward. But his strength was gone. Arms spasming, he fell to the floor and lay there without moving.

"Guptas," said the old demon, kicking at him, and Marilyn could hear a note of regret in his voice. "Guptas the Fool, who could have ruled the world."

Raising his eyes, he glared at Marilyn. "You ruined it all," he whispered bitterly. "I think it's time for you to die."

Marilyn pressed back against the rim of the forge. The old demon stepped over Guptas and took her by the neck. His claws began to sink into her skin.

"That's enough," said a voice behind them.

The demon turned around, then began to scream.

Marilyn looked up in astonishment.

Among the litter of demons, looking down at them, stood Suleiman, father of Guptas.

"Give me the amulet," he said. His voice was quiet, strong, gentle, ancient, filled with sorrow. He extended his arm. Marilyn reached up and laid the amulet in his palm. It seemed oddly tiny in his great hand.

"No!" screamed the old demon. "Great king, do not do this. No! No! No!"

"Silence!" said Suleiman.

Closing his massive fingers over the amulet, he spoke softly, in some ancient language. A great crack of something like thunder reverberated through the chamber.

The old demon vanished.

Smoke curled from between the king's fingers. He opened his hand, gazed at the amulet for a moment, then tossed it into the forge.

The explosion knocked Marilyn to her knees.

The flames returned to normal. By their flickering light she watched as the king knelt to gather his battered son into his arms.

Guptas stirred in his grasp. "Father," he whispered.

"I should have loved you better," said the king sadly as he cradled Guptas against his chest.

After a moment the king lifted his head to look at Marilyn. Tears shimmered at the corners of his eyes. "Thank you," he said softly. "Without your trust, my son would have been doomed forever."

He looked around the room and spotted Kyle, who was quietly trying to bear the agony of his many wounds.

"Tell your friend to come before me," said Suleiman. The shadow of a smile flickered over his face. "And bring me your cat, as well."

Mystified, Marilyn gestured to Kyle, who had forced himself to his knees.

"I can't," he whispered. "I can't move."

"I'll help," she said. "Just wait."

She limped to the wall where Brick lay and lifted him gently from the floor. He was still breathing, but his body was badly broken. He opened one eye and tried to yowl in protest. The sound was pathetically weak.

"Poor baby," whispered Marilyn. Cradling the cat gently in her arms, she went to Kyle. "Put your arm on my shoulder," she said, kneeling beside him.

He struggled to his feet.

Together they crossed to the king.

Suleiman knelt and laid Guptas gently down beside him. "This much I can do for you," he said softly to Marilyn. He took Brick from her arms and held the cat cupped in his enormous hands. He closed his eyes. Brick stiffened for a moment, yowled almost in anger, then sat up, blinking, absurdly small on the king's palm.

He looked up, yowled this time in fright, and jumped back into Marilyn's arms.

Suleiman smiled. "Now you," he said to Kyle.

Kyle stepped forward. The king took him in his great arms. Like Brick, Kyle yelled out. And, like Brick, his wounds were healed. He touched himself in amazement. "Thank you," he said awkwardly.

Suleiman held Marilyn and healed her, too; healed the burns, the slash of the ax, the bruises that covered her body. And, a little, he healed the wounds of her spirit, the fear that lingered within.

After he set her down, he gathered Guptas into his arms once more. The demon stirred, then opened his eyes. With an effort that was clearly painful, he reached out his hand to Marilyn.

She stepped forward and took it. The scaly flesh was warm and dry, surprisingly pleasant to the touch.

"Thank you," he whispered. "Thank you for trusting me."

Marilyn squeezed his hand. "What will happen to him now?" she asked, looking up at the king.

"He will come to be with me." Suleiman looked around the room. "As for you, you should all go home now. Some of you have a lot to learn," he added, looking pointedly at Eldred Cooley.

"I'd love to go home," said Marilyn. "But how do we get there without Guptas?"

The king looked at her in astonishment. "What do you have a cat for?" he asked.

And then he was gone, taking his son with him.

Epilogue

Marilyn sat between Kyle and Alicia at the funeral home, listening to the preacher talk about Zenobia. She looked around. She still couldn't believe she and Kyle were in one piece, much less that they had managed to get this place back in shape in time to get out while it was still dark last night.

Getting Zenobia's body back into her coffin had been the worst part, of course. Once they had managed that, Marilyn had tried to arrange the flowers so no one would notice that the amulet was missing.

Marilyn looked up and suppressed a smile. Zenobia was sitting on the end of her coffin, looking at the minister as if she couldn't believe her ears.

"They always spout such nonsense," she had said

to Marilyn on the way home last night. "I can't wait to hear what he has to say about me."

Now, seeing that Marilyn was looking at her, Zenobia mouthed a single word: "Baloney!"

Marilyn snorted, then tried to turn the sound into a sob.

Alicia dug her in the ribs. Kyle squeezed her hand. They all stood for the hymn.

Twelve hours later Marilyn was sitting in her bed, telling Brick what a great cat he was for getting them all back, when Zenobia walked through her closed door.

Marilyn smiled. "I was hoping you would come."

"It's just to say good-bye."

Marilyn frowned. "Do you have to go?"

Zenobia nodded. "Afraid so. There's so much to do. I can't tell you all about it. But trust me, it's exciting."

"The last adventure?" asked Marilyn, trying to smile.

"The biggest," said Zenobia. "If they would just let me have a cigar, I'd be in Heaven."

ABOUT THE AUTHOR

BRUCE COVILLE has been scaring people ever since he was born and the doctor screamed, "Oh my God! What's *that?*"

His parents were nearly as terrified.

His teachers are still nervous wrecks.

All that took place back in the totally terrifying decade of the 1950s, in and around Syracuse, New York.

When Bruce became a teenager his grandfather put him to work digging graves in the local cemetery.

His high school's official colors were orange and black.

He spent as much time as possible watching monster movies, reading "Famous Monsters of Filmland" magazine, and scaring himself by imagining what might be underneath his bed.

Given all that, we have to ask you: is it any surprise he writes this kind of book?

Mr. Coville now lives with his wife, his youngest child, and their three weird cats in a rather odd brick house on a hill in Syracuse.

He hasn't dug a grave in years.

Or so he says.